SHADOWS ON THE MIRROR

FRANCES FYFIELD

sphere

SPHERE

First published in Great Britain by William Heinemann Ltd in 1989
Published in paperback by Mandarin in 1990
Published in ebook in 2012 by Sphere
This paperback edition published in 2019 by Sphere

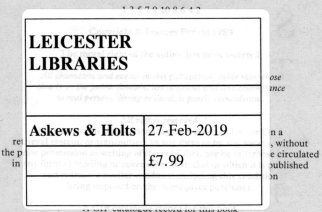

is available from the British Library.

ISBN 978-0-7515-7751-8

Typeset in Plantin by M Rules
Printed and bound in Great Britain by
Clays Ltd, Elcograf S.p.A.

Papers used by Sphere are from well-managed forests
and other responsible sources.

Sphere
An imprint of
Little, Brown Book Group
Carmelite House
50 Victoria Embankment
London EC4Y 0DZ

An Hachette UK Company
www.hachette.co.uk

www.littlebrown.co.uk

To
Sylvia Norton,
Jenny Jones, Martyn Woodnutt,
Michael Kew and the other colleagues
who make working life bearable

FOREWORD

He had loved her, she knew, in his vile, obsessive way, but she wished he had loved in a manner she understood. If he had ever loved her in some ordinary sense, he might have been here now, or she might not ... But she could not cope with his kind of love or see herself as pet or instrument, could not live with being ugly.

The child laughing at her was the end. Politely she had ignored it, walked on and seen her face in the window, the same face she had tried to ignore in most mirrors, disgusted at itself, but smiling to make it worse. Then she saw her own reflection in the waters of the quay, hovering and hideous by the boats, lower than life, and told herself she had brought her arse to anchor here. Even without an audience, she had apologised automatically to Charles for the inelegant expression: he had never liked her crudity except in bed.

Then she went home for the pills.

Wherever she looked, she caught herself smiling at

passers-by, the way she always smiled in that other life. No good him saying they don't notice the stitches, only the smile, like a lighthouse beacon: he would not believe it, nor did she. Charles had married her for her beauty, which he had made all ways ugly, and she could not, would not live with it.

The final hope was revenge. Messages in cellophane in her purse and on her body bringing home to him, like ships in bottles, some sort of disgrace to damn him to hell. She could see from her face now how much she had loved him and how much she hated him now. Something the mirror and she could understand. She did not believe such a life could be redeemed as she paddled across the low tide and walked towards the blue distance, unsteady but determined. The man, distracted by the boy who had laughed in her face, thought she was drunk to walk like that, lurching and slightly slow. The tide was well turned, forcing her to wade through the water in the late evening sun. They assumed she would come back, lie down with her hideous face and sleep. She looked so tired.

Next day, Sunday morning, summery, and away they were, down the creeks off the coast at Merton-on-Sea. He rowed out down the creeks with the screaming child in the boat. Born here and why not, can't complain, mad if he did, and he wasn't that. No cloud in the sky, except this beloved step-son who couldn't stand the sea. Silly little sod, about eight years old and cried like a baby whenever he was taken out in the boat. The sky was full of his wild sobbing, but they had Grandma's house on the quay, he and the boy's mother. He could not afford a child who did not like water. They slept each night with the sea, and the boy would have to learn.

But not this one, he wouldn't do nothing to order, not ever. Put him in the boat, and he screamed fit to bust, so it had to be done again and again, kill or cure, poor little bastard, hates it, don't know why. The new wife said it was the flood, when the tide put the boats right into the high street shops at midnight, and the boy lost his dad after a night howling on the roof, waiting for the storm to die. The new father had loved this woman too much and too long not to try. He'd have loved her with ten children, let alone this funny little brute. There was another on the way, light on the horizon, apart from the boy screaming and breathless, frightened of everything, making him feel like a monster. 'C'mon, you little monkey,' he muttered. 'I love you better than all the world, and if you think I'll like the new one better, you're dafter than I thought. Stop crying now, good lad. This is where you get out in the warm and paddle, and stop screeching. There now. Not so bad is it?'

He wanted the boy to love the creeks as he loved them. When the tide went out, water crept away through all these channels, leaving a trickle of rivers, with good shallow pools for swimming, safe as houses until the tide came roaring back and filled the gullies. When the tide was low, there was a playground of soft and sinking sand; when high, a riot of swift, deep water.

The boy recovered instantly as soon as he was out of the boat. He would run around a corner of the bank towards the nearest pool, forgetting the torture of the journey completely, singing and playing while the borrowed father dug for bait. Peaceful for the moment, basking in sun without wind in the snug seclusion of the channels. The man sighed with relief, pulled the boat further on to the bank, and sighed again with pleasure. Until he saw her.

If she hadn't been dead, lying with her gob full of sand, he could have killed her, simply for lying there waiting to give the child a heart attack. He'd always been worried they'd find a dead dog or something out there, something to frighten the wits out of the boy just as he was beginning to make some kind of progress. She looked like a bundle of rags, hands twisted in the heather, silly bitch. Sea must have come in over her and gone down again, leaving her covered with mud and sand. Once he knew it was a body, he'd chucked water at its face. Red hair she had, terrible scars, and Christ, he recognised her. She was the one the boy had laughed at only yesterday while his ma cuffed him. He'd go mad if he saw her now, sharp-eyed little bugger. Mad and frightened, he'd be, then there'd be the asthma, panic and rows. He looked up quickly for the child, heard him down by the pool, singing softly to himself, hardly out of sight. Noise was muffled in the channels.

Get rid of her. Nothing else for it. He could not let the child see. The banks were soft and easy, there was a shovel for bait in the boat and the muddy sand turned softly on the blade as he dug in the panic of haste, sweating himself like a pig to cover her in before the boy came back, soaking his clothes and gritting his teeth as he dragged the damp salty mass of her into a deep grave. He weighted her down before he slung the slodgy mud back on to her, closing his eyes and ears to the impact of its landing. What else to do? She had wanted to be found, that much was obvious, but not at his expense. It would take a tide or ten to shift her from there: next spring maybe. Maybe never. Sorry, lady. Silly bitch, you stay where you damn well are, stay down. I got my own to care for, he said, and this boy's done enough crying.

The woman called Elisabeth was buried without trace or ceremony. In the bedroom of his London home, a husband twitched and dozed full of the last nightmares. I loved you, my Porphyria, he told himself, but I shall find another.

Houses stirred into early evening. A fat lawyer and a young widow went out to dinner. Life went on as the hungry tide came back and covered the mound of earth, flattening it into innocence.

CHAPTER ONE

In the days before he had ever heard of Charles Tysall, and on the date when a certain scarred lady disappeared, Malcolm Cook was a very fat man indeed, but when he reared up in court with an energetic grace quite at odds with the huge size of him, the audience forgot to laugh. While they were expecting the idiot to overbalance his bulk, tickle himself, and tell jokes, his mellifluous voice was not only a surprise but the first premonition of trouble for those who knew him slightly enough to believe that the prosecution had fielded a buffoon. He was genial and twinkling, an old young man, so harmless when his fat laugh echoed round the foyer, a man with whom a defendant could feel safe, until, armed with his voice and his uncanny intelligence, he asked for his answers. They were kind, compelling eyes, betraying knowledge of exactly what it was like to be cast aside like the man in the dock, whatever he had done. The accused betrayed themselves to him by confident lies, tripping over details, looking at the fat man and forgetting where they were, keeping nothing but the dignity he would never steal from them. In the courtroom, Malcolm Cook, Senior Crown Prosecutor, was a man of charisma, compassion and great forensic skill, a gentle giant with powerful weapons. Everywhere else, he was regarded as a perfect clown.

It was beyond doubt that he was gross in size, but there was a finesse hidden in the bulk of it he was never encouraged to show, and certainly not in present company, as far as Sarah Fortune could tell. Bright brown glance, looking at women with eyes which knew they were not looking back, determined against embarrassment, blanked against longing. Malcolm's stories were famous, told in a dozen accents, and as for his antics, they made a party all on their own. A curiosity, with merely borrowed membership of the human race, freakish good value, everyone forgave the way he looked. Belinda Smythe would never seat as many as eight at her gatherings of lawyers, accountants, architects and assorted spouses without him being one of them, since his mere presence ensured success. Pound for pound, Malcolm Cook was worth the feeding since he provided a shoulder for weeping ladies, chest for pummelling children, mouth for laughing and merely sociable kisses, big clever teddy for the whole world. And he could drink. The legendary capacity was first joke of the evening: 'We've been down to the warehouse for you, Malcolm, here's your crate.' 'Thanks very much, see you're as mean as ever.' A benign exchange of seasoned insults, tokens of pleasure to meet him, all smiles and relief:

he would see to the evening's entertainment. Sarah watched him closely, wondering if she was wrong to sense a kindred spirit, another outsider like herself, being used on a hostess ego-trip, someone who had arrived for dinner as an alternative to loneliness. Imagination had run riot in the six months of her altered status. She was sick of being invited out of duty and knew this was the last time she would accept. She tried and failed to dismiss her curiosity for the haunted man who laughed too much.

'Malckie?' shrieked Belinda, sensing from the kitchen the comparative lull which signified his absence from the room beyond when his presence was crucial. 'Where are you?'

'He's gone to see the children,' said Sarah, dutiful guest making salad-dressing.

'What's he want to do that for? Damn the man, we're ready to eat. Go and fetch him, Sarah, won't you?' Sing for your supper, Malcolm; Belinda was leaving nothing to chance. Sarah went, grateful her role in the guest hierarchy was less onerous than his. It was far easier to look pretty, please the people and run errands, the last done most willingly for the excuse of brief escapes. She was sent to look for the warm-up man who had left his audience to wither without him; he must hurry back or they would miss him.

She found him upstairs, squatting at the bedside of a snuffling three-year-old, his stomach and chest meeting bulging thighs while the child giggled softly at the jowled faces he pulled. 'Noo, no, wait.' Conspiratorial whispers. 'Can you do this one?' 'Which one?' 'Like this.' Eyes pulled down by one thumb and fourth finger, nose pushed up and sideways by the other thumb . . . 'Ugghh!' 'Good, isn't it?' 'Triffic, show me how . . .' Sarah saw them both in the mirror, lit by the night-light left to comfort the child, a huge grown man lost in playing, the child transfixed with concentration. Each in his element, herself in the mirror, the silhouette of an interfering adult. She did not want to stop him; happiest in clowning to an audience who knew him with better instincts than those downstairs, but his dark eyes caught her brief movement, the barely perceptible warning gesture of hers which said, don't stop, you're doing fine, I did not mean to interrupt, and at once the face of him showed weary anger before a resigned smile. He turned to the child with a warmer smile, and tucked her arms below the sheet.

'Must go, honey, supper's ready.'

'Will you come back later, Malcolm, promise?'

'Promise, but you know how Mummy fusses about the food.'

There was more giggling. 'Give me a kiss, Malcolm, please.'

'Ah.' Aware of his audience, he paused theatrically. 'I can't resist that, you know I can't.'

The child threw her arms round his neck and hugged for dear life. Malcolm's upper arm where the golden head was buried hid her completely in the breadth of it. Sarah thought of King Kong with his tiny princess, ridiculous, sad, but complete for the moment. The eyes meeting Sarah's over the blonde hair in his arms issued a brief challenge before the grown-up mask returned. 'See?' he joked for the adult not the child. 'Beautiful women find me irresistible.' She turned away from them and left, embarrassed by her presence at the scene of genuine affection and equally disturbed by the change her presence provoked. Next time she looked he would be one of the bosom buddies, a proper guest, one of the pack.

'He'll be back,' she told Belinda briefly. 'And by the way, what a gorgeous daughter you have.' The mother had her hands full, not thinking of children.

'Zoe? Yes, she's sweet. Adores Malckie of course, so does our son. There'll be ructions in the morning if he's spoken to one and not the other. He'll have to come round again. We all adore Malckie.'

But you don't, Sarah thought. You don't even begin to see him. You're giving houseroom to all that bulk simply because he entertains; you have no idea of what he is, what he does, or what he feels. He is here through loneliness and because he loves your children. If you were a true friend you'd put him on a diet rather than insist he eat even more than all the others, while you make him play to your gallery, damn your bloody silliness. And why do I come to your house when I don't even like you? Because you're my husband's friends, and because, like Malcolm, I'm useful. No, that isn't fair, I know it isn't fair, it was my choice I'm here, no one made me. Not your fault, but I've just seen something of big fat Malcolm you might not have seen, and I'll bet your daughter knows him a damn sight better than you. Sad man, but not pathetic. She could not move him from her mind.

Belinda and Martin Smythe were living happily ever after in the house he had converted from a mid-Hampstead ruin. Each visit there involved another guided tour, since some

11

aspect of the house was bound to have changed. It moved and altered like a living thing, first a conservatory appeared, then another bedroom, then an attic created out of roof space, signs of admirable energy, but she could never quite understand why she didn't feel comfortable. The whole thing was violent and superficial self-advertisement and so were the owners. Sarah's husband had loved it; now it was time for dividing the ways. But she was here now; she should be grateful for the irritating insensitivity of their generosity.

And she wasn't bored, simply disturbed: no one was bored with Malcolm around, court jester, delighting them all with self-mockery.

'What do you do?' Someone asked him the inevitable party question.

'Obvious, isn't it?' he replied with the infectious grin, pirouetting on the carpet, mincing his steps with one hand on huge hip. 'Male model for Aquascutum double-breasted. When I'm not doing swimwear.' Shrieks of laughter. He was a gifted mimic with his extravagant gestures, tossing imaginary locks out of his eyes, assuming the distant gimlet glare of the romantic hero, tripping over his own feet. 'But when I grow up . . . ' – they waited with bated breath – 'I shall pose for Henry Moore. Why hide a perfect body like this?' Belinda was priming him for more. 'Where did you get that suit, Malc?' she said, pointing to his well-worn garment. 'That, my dear, was specially imported. It is the produce of wool from a thousand Falkland sheep who shrugged their fleece simultaneously as soon as they knew the size of the order . . . ' And so it went on until Malcolm's antics had welded a group of relative strangers into an audience who could talk among themselves. 'Another drink, Malckie?' 'Oh, please, just give me the bottle and a straw ...' Outrageous, he encouraged them all to their party pieces, stroking performers as he left them the stage, assuring all present that though they might feel foolish, he would be worse.

Sarah was nurturing a resentment she knew was unjustified, watching Malcolm Cook with a liking which grew in proportion to the loneliness of him, which glared towards anyone observant enough to see it. She saw the fat, asthmatic little boy he had been, standing on the sidelines as he did now, making up stories and pulling faces for attention, fighting his own demons. She liked him with a furious and defensive liking, intensely angry with him for clinging to acceptance where it was offered at the price of acting the fool. This much she had gathered by the time the sweet course was placed in front of Malckie in magnificent creamy entirety with a teasing flourish of stunning unkindness by Martin. 'All yours, old man. Thought you were wasting away ...' 'So kind,' said Malcolm, 'but I always take cheese first ...' The table rocked with well-fed mirth, and Sarah squirmed for the victim reacting to his cue, taking his poison. The man needed intravenous confidence, something to make him love himself. 'I know what you need,' Sarah told herself, ' ... and I should like to provide it, by way of experiment.' Not a whole cure, but a start perhaps.

Tutting for baby-sitters, looking at watches, everyone far later than meant, satisfying for smug hosts. Again, Malcolm had slipped away unnoticed to honour promises to sleeping

13

children, returned for goodbyes lasting even later, reluctant farewells in the blast of wintry cold from the glass door. 'Ah well, cab for me,' Malcolm was saying between assuring Belinda how well he had fared. 'I'll give you a lift,' said Sarah. 'No need, really no need. Think I'll jog home and come back for breakfast.' 'I'll give you a lift,' she repeated. 'My pleasure.' He found a final joke irresistible. 'Send out a search party for us,' he said, 'after three days . . . '

In the draughty doorway of the house, the place for the last and best intimacies of the evening, Belinda fussily took Sarah aside in a sudden, guilty sympathy. Perhaps she should not have made it so clear that Sarah was a duty guest, invited on the coat-tails of a dead husband.

'Sarah. Haven't had the chance, you know how it is, but how are you really? I'm so sorry . . . we're still devastated, but you know where we are if ever we can help . . . Must be awful being on your own, how do you cope? What on earth do you find to do with yourself these days?' She was surprised by the sudden sparkle in the blue eyes, the amused appreciation in the ironic smile of all her obvious condescension.

'I manage, thank you,' said Sarah.

Hilly Hampstead spun with brittle ice. 'Tell me the way to Kentish Town,' she asked, concentrating through misty windows on the road ahead. 'I'm lost here.' 'What? Oh, left at the bottom, then right. I'm lost anywhere.' Not joking, distracted, the first sign of the evening's strain. Followed by silence. Malcolm looked at her smooth profile as he had been looking all evening, the slim elegance of her tucked into the seat, her round bosom parted and emphasised by the seat-belt. Then looked away, sick with longing to touch the thick red hair. Half hidden by coat, he could picture the demure dress she had worn, skimming slim knees descending to pretty ankles, soft-flowing stuff over firm, muscular hips. Fit, he supposed. Athletic, calmly authoritative, competent and anathema, like all beautiful young women who were the stuff of dreams erotic and otherwise, never pursued by a man of his dimensions but very lovely all the same. Likeable, attractive on sight, gentler than them all, but like every one of her kind, could not be allowed to see this sickening twist of longing in the clown hunched into her small car. Would never return such a look or volunteer to touch him. No one ever touched him, and he never importuned. Malcolm Cook felt himself a leper with women like this, but it did not stop him wanting.

'Here?' The car lurched to a halt and he fumbled with the handle, suddenly clumsy.

'I'd like some coffee if I may.' He hadn't heard right, a humble request in a calm, clear voice. 'Yes, of course, come on up.' Hearing his own voice sulky with surprise, then firmer. 'Yes, of course. I should have offered, but I thought . . . ' An illuminating smile on her face, full of forgiving mischief. ' . . . You thought I would want to offload you as soon as possible. But I don't. And I need coffee.'

There were books by the thousand indoors, pictures by the dozen, solid furniture which seemed to correspond with his own weight and size. A man's womanly touch, clearly distinguishable from a woman's touch, existed in the kind of austere comfort produced. Small and tidy, the lair of

15

an isolated creature who exerted rigid control over his life, dared not encourage visitors for the contrasts in their departures, and clung to his home for the rock of peace it offered. Perhaps she was mad, perhaps she imagined it all, but from the moment she had watched him lumber into action like a well-trained and baited dancing bear manacled by mysterious grief, she had been drawn to this loneliness and knew she would not leave it untouched.

'Music?' he asked. She nodded, watched him fuss awkwardly with unaccustomed hospitality, unwind marginally and heavily on the sofa beside her. It was the only seating in the room, which left him without the alternative he would have half preferred, to sit outside touching distance.

'May I ask you something?'

'Of course.' Only slightly flustered, but flattered. The cold had brought a glow to her pale skin and the eyes were enormous.

'Why do you let them use you like that? You know exactly what I mean.'

He looked at the clear intelligence of the face, haloed by the red hair, began to bluster and decided not. His large head shook, puzzled and confused by the question he had often asked himself.

'I exist to be jester,' he said slowly. 'What else can I do?'

Abruptly he rose, poured a brandy from a decanter and handed her a glass without invitation. She took it and sipped, waiting. He was hesitant, wanting by now to explain it all, believing her sympathy, ashamed of himself for beginning to talk.

16

'... I suppose ... I suppose ... Why on earth do you want to know?'

'Just accept that I do want to know. Go on.'

'I'll have to simplify it then.'

'As simple as you like.'

'Not easy all the same. I'm fat, you see. Enormous. Ugly.'

'Not ugly. Who told you that?'

'The mirror tells me that. My mother told me that. Other women's eyes tell me that. I have always been gross: glandular baby, fatty child, ungainly student, fat man. So I immerse myself in criminal law, my work, which makes it worse. But being fat is my trademark, has its uses I suppose, and I don't know how to change it. I must make something semi-dignified from it. So, I make people laugh; relieves the monotony of existence, gives me a measure of acceptance. And if you say, lose the fat, I will say there will always be a fat man in me whatever I do. I daren't try in case it makes no difference.'

'Who comes close to you? Who do you tell?'

'Don't be silly. No one till now. The way I am? My world is far too competitive to confide in men, and I can't trouble women although I prefer their company ... '

'Why not?'

He looked at her. 'Why not? Oh, come now, I'd always want more than friendship, although the women to date have never offered it. Since you're so keen on the pursuit of my humiliation, you may as well know why no woman would ever want me. She'd get lost in all this flesh, and I would have to watch her shrink away, with me dying of shame but

17

still joking. I couldn't bear it, so bloody unfair to ask. Am I making this sound self-pitying enough?'

'No, but there is a hint of it. I never heard anything so silly. What do you do, shove the whole world to one side because of an extra bit of flesh? What would you do if you didn't have legs?'

'Beg, on my elbows, to be taken seriously sometimes. Or just to be taken.'

She laughed, close to him, innocently close as she stroked his wide eyebrows, tracing the arches with a finger. 'Fine eyes, good skin, thick head of hair. You've a lovely head, you know.'

'Don't.' Part embarrassment, some particle of gratitude made him hug her, conscious of the bulk of himself, if only to make her stop.

'I'm not being foolish, you are. Forever seeing yourself as you think other people see you, imperfect first, as if there was nothing there which couldn't be weighed in kilos. What an idiot, always asking yourself the same question, "Speaking as an outsider, boy, what do you think of the human race?" Not a lot.'

'Enough,' he said quietly. 'Don't confuse self-pity with honesty. Look at me. I'm disgusting. I'm the object of revulsion in half the human race, and I can't even blame them. I think that explains it all.'

'I'm looking,' she said. 'I've been looking all the time.' And I like outsiders like me, she added to herself. They make me feel at home.

Malcolm Cook, clown *extraordinaire*, stopped the tears

inside his own eyes, swallowed the last of his brandy. Intent on the effort of self-control he failed to notice the swift movement which brought her closer. 'You idiot,' she said. 'You silly, silly idiot.' So softly said, he scarcely heard with her hand caressing the back of his neck, relaxing his whole spine, then touching his face, her fingers through his hair smoothing and soothing. He had begun his small protest before she began her kiss. 'Sshh, sshh, my lovely, stay still, don't send me away, not now.' Her mouth on his own with a sweet brandy smell, gentle, his tongue exploring the taste, his hand on her breast where she had placed it, moving, wondering, feeling the fluid flesh beneath the cloth and her nipple beneath his fingers. 'Please,' he whispered. 'No pity please.' Her thumb stroked the crease between his eyes, her lips brushed his forehead. 'No pity at all,' she replied. 'No judgement either. Stop thinking of yourself as a freak. You're nothing of the kind. I do this because it pleases me to do so.' Malcolm did not speak, looked at the calm grey eyes and believed. Slowly she unbuttoned the modest dress, kneeling beside him, touched with his tongue, he pulled her towards him as her hands pulled away his clothes. 'Sarah, Sarah, Sarah.' He had known her name but never said it, spoke it now like a litany, lifted her to the floor and himself alongside her. Miraculously naked, flesh upon flesh, tingling and weightless, aware and ashamed, stunned into agonising life, he wanted her to stop, but never to stop, helpless with wanting, conscious of warmth, enveloping affection, rhythmic movement of her hips against his own until the dim light of the room faded, everything faded in the mounting wave of sensation. Hold me, Sarah, hold me, please, I can't help it. Don't stop.

Calm. A quiet popping sound from the fire above the noise of his own breath, her head resting against his chest with one large hand still pressing her into himself, the other stroking her hair. Agony of relief, gratitude, apology, Sarah, Sarah. 'Sorry,' he mumbled. 'Not much fun for you.' The head raised above his own was flushed, tousled, alive with an impish grin. 'That,' she said, rubbing his nose with the tip of her own, kissing his eyes, 'was the beginning. Or are you going to send me home now?'

'No,' said Malcolm. 'I'm not.'

Talking towards dawn, he had never known how easy it was to talk when touching, how peaceful to speak of unmentionable things to one who listened by instinct, could even understand how he had arrived, by various routes, to stand on the outside of the world as a constant and lonely observer. In turn he absorbed the untold history of Sarah, the lost child, the emptiness. Two outsiders, finding truth in nakedness: absolute trust. He could scarcely believe how simple it was. Then, when they made love for the second time, he believed before he slept he had conquered the world, had heard her cry out in a kind of joy. He had done that, made her body leap and rear before she had cried out, convulsed around him. He had caused that pleasure, he and that great big body. Idiot, she had said again, the affection turning insult into compliment. Idiot to doubt yourself, now you know better, and he was proud, slept with his arm tucked beneath her. Hug me, she said, my lovely lover, and huge ungainly Malcolm Cook hugged after hours

20

of talking, no longer afraid, and, no longer a freak, slept the sleep of a child. Then opened his eyes to find himself alone.

Bow Street on Monday morning, prosecutor Court One, Mr Cook. 'Thirty on the list, sir.' Street traders, hot-dog stalls, touts and drunks, easy. Three for soliciting prostitution, fighting the evidence. 'Them three's contesting, sir, but we can't find the papers. Better ask for an adjournment, sir.' Malcolm looked at the bold and tired faces of the three at the back, one of them bulky, pointing at him and laughing, one thin, one blank and black. He remembered the note left on his kitchen table in Sarah's clear hand. 'Being fat isn't the point. Being you is the point and, I'm telling you, nothing is lacking. You're a marvellous man, better than anyone else. You don't need me, you only need you. Please don't try and find me; you must change yourself, or it will not count for anything. Besides, you're on the way up, and I'm definitely on the way down. Just love yourself as much as I did. I shan't ever forget you.' Malcolm remembered the searing of grief, and the image of himself in the mirror, fat and stricken, half-naked. He made himself a promise: he would find her when he was a different man, a thinner, more dignified man, worth the loving of a woman of such peculiar and glorious qualities, but before then he would change simply because she had made him feel alive, was the first who had made him want to change. Clichéd thought, he made himself smile at it: this is only the first day of life.

In the meantime remember fairness, his hallmark along with his size.

'If we have no papers,' he said to the gaoler, 'put the ladies up first. I'll be offering no evidence. Then we can let them go. Who the hell are we to judge?'

There it was. Compassion always far more important than duty, living better than dying. Time to alter. Love did that, and he would always love her, for what she was and what she had done. He would find her when he had completed the revolution she had started; find her and love her although all he knew was her name. Then, looking up briefly at the ladies of the night, freed from the dock with squawks of relief, he wondered what Sarah had meant by saying she was on the way down, thought of the words with a flash of anxious intuition quickly dismissed as he lumbered to his feet for the next cue.

CHAPTER TWO

Within the next two years, Malcolm dreamed of many things, including his stepfather's office, but he never visited it, and knew better than to make inquiries about the progress of that empire, since any question sparked a row. Not many solicitors' premises, even bigger city types, were quite as sumptuous as these, and none bore a sign as ostentatiously discreet, 'Matthewson, Carman and Company, Solicitors', very small lettering on an enormous brass plaque. Nothing flashy, please, Matthewson had said, confronting the interior designer lady. Normally it was the sort of thing Ernest Matthewson left to his wife. His house was a mass of birds and flowers, curtains and chairs full of them. He could not see why the office décor mattered. Clients like Charles Tysall would not notice the colour of the walls, it would only make them suspicious about what was being done with their fees. Whenever Ernest, Malcolm's stepfather, thought of Charles

Tysall, he felt sick and pointless, and nothing as banal as his surroundings was going to help.

Matthewson had built his practice on common sense, pats on shoulders, a large handkerchief, tea, sympathy and stiff drinks, and above all the ability to keep a secret, but success had exacted its peculiar punishment. Sofas like squashed elephants, forty-five solicitors and only one of them he liked. Whatever had happened to the place where he started three ulcers and one heart attack ago, God knew; he didn't. He was lonely and he missed his stepson more than ever, not daily, but hourly. There were only a few minutes a day, faced with the ghastly luxury of the reception, when he knew why Malcolm preferred his darker regions.

'It's not the same,' he would mutter to Penelope. 'Not the same at all.' Mrs Matthewson, known as Pen to her friends, would try to forestall the depression by planning an extra course on the evening's menu, food being the only panacea she knew. *Moules marinières*, perhaps. No, not in this mood. A sweetener the other end: *mousse au chocolat*, delivered to him without pointing out he had no real choice. For the firm, she meant, hadn't had any choice in a long time.

'That woman in Commercial is awful,' he would say. 'As bad as the bloody decor. How can anyone as frightful earn so much?' Pen would bring him a drink and suggest that cash was not always acquired by the same means as his own charm and common sense. 'Not like you,' she would say. 'Not your flair.' Fondling the back of his neck in the same way she fondled the space behind the ears of their cat, preferring Ernest's soft and bristly stubble, the creased warmth of it.

24

'Not like you. They can't all be so lucky. Her work needs brains. I mean, law does these days.' He did not take offence, knowing flattery was meant. 'At least they're all respectable,' Penelope added, by way of comfort. 'I wish they bloody well weren't,' he shouted. 'Stuffed shirts, every one. Thirty-going-on-ninety.' She soothed him. 'Not like Sarah Fortune,' he would say. 'No, dear, not like Sarah,' she would reply, stiffening her back, pretending to Ernest she resented such eulogies of praise which might follow for the widow Fortune. Then she would stride towards her kitchen in the direction of the good smells, walking across twenty-five feet of carpet with her plump tread, smiling to herself. Let him fantasise about Sarah Fortune. It did him good to think she might resent his praising Sarah Fortune. Penelope knew better and it did not do to let Ernest know he had been so thoroughly discussed. She also knew that the most romantic assignation Ernest ever had with this lady was to play cards with her in the basement of the office when no one but the caretaker was looking. Penelope and Sarah had found one another at the first Christmas party Sarah had attended in the new office. Between them, discreetly, they had got tiddly Ernest home. Penelope had squared up to Sarah. 'My husband is always talking about you,' she had begun.

'Is he really? I'm flattered. I'm very fond of him. And he's safe with me.' Then in a lowered voice, with a disarming smile of conspiracy, 'You see, Mrs Matthewson, he and I share something. We're the only lawyers here who don't know any law ... we make it up as we go along ... sometimes we have to confess, as well as hide. Then we have a drink.'

Pen wished she had a daughter like Sarah Fortune, instead of the son. No, not instead of the son, as well as him. Penelope knew what Sarah did in Ernest's office, inspired guesswork and a few other things. They had discussed it, taking their turn with Ernest's whisky long after Ernest had fallen asleep that Christmas. Penelope knew when a girl could be trusted and when not. She had never told as much to anyone, or felt as safe.

Pen stirred the sauce. Ernest had turned on the music, a sure sign of recovery. At least this evening he was not going to dwell on the other two sources of grief: his stepson Malcolm, who so adamantly refused to join the firm or have anything to do with it, for reasons Ernest could not understand, and the client, Charles Tysall, who told poor Ernest the sort of secrets Ernest could never share, making him physically ill. Guilt, that was Ernest's problem. Couldn't bear to think he had failed, and when the guilt struck, thought Penelope, he ceases to judge them at all. Becomes immobile, like an animal hypnotised.

Eight-fifteen on the Rothbury Estate, finest statement of Victorian values for the poor, despised, these days, by most of them. Built around a well with a scrub of kicked-up lawn, ancient white brick, small windows, Noise was echoing as the last of Joan's children clattered down the steps. 'Wait for me. Wait for meeee ... ' Jack's voice drifting back, forever plaintive. She sighed and wished she had not shouted. Time to go to the office of Matthewson and become secretary to Miss Fortune, rather than mother to this brat-pack. She tidied the room in a flurry of hate, pushing dirty clothes in a sack, food in the bin, dishes in the sink, leaving the beds and the washing. Mustn't grumble: just think if Ted were here, the mess would be worse. Ted Plumb, divorced husband, lived like a tornado, could reduce a room to a dump within minutes, and somewhere in the muddle, there would be a whisky bottle. Joan sat down on the sofa, suddenly winded by the thought. No, if Ted was still with them, they wouldn't be living here, would they? If not in a house, at least they'd have a police flat with one more room and a caretaker. The bloody Commissioner made his officers look after their families, even officers like Ted, and if they wouldn't, he did, in a manner of speaking.

But all of them were beyond such protection now. Ted had put it behind them. Disgraced, sacked, living in a grotty bedsit, God knows where, still with a bottle for company, and Lord alone knows what else.

'You really did it proper, didn't you, Ted?' Joan scowled into her mirror, adding a row of beads to the rest of the colours. 'You really blew the whole thing. Us, in a half-condemned council flat no one else wants, and you up shit creek. And now you want to kiss and make up. Well, sod you.'

She pushed the hat on her head, twisted the stocking sideways round her ankle so the holes would not show, picked up her bright red bag and slammed out of the door. Wait till she told Sarah what the bugger had done. Sarah would laugh and, despite herself, she would be made to feel better however much she might resent it. She might just turn up and offer to take Jack on Sunday, give her a break, the way she sometimes did. Odd woman doing that for nothing; why the hell should she? But she did. At least, Joan thought, I've got a job. I hate bloody typing, but at least I don't work for some bloke. At least I work for a woman, even if she is too bloody clever by half.

Teetering on high heels, adjusting the shoulder bag, Joan was thinking hard. Get to Tescos at lunchtime, beans, spuds, underpants for John, socks for Jack, soap, and they all needed shoes. £19.99 a pair, kids' shoes . . . They needed everything, and what had he carried in under his arm as a peace-offering for the first visit in three months? A dog, a bloody dog, not even a puppy, probably stolen. A relic of a Christmas present. The kids had loved it. Joan had exploded.

'What the hell am I supposed to do with it?' Hissing, wresting it away from Jack, shoving it back into Ted's arms. 'Three floors up, no money for clothes, let alone dog food.'

'I thought the kids would like it,' he said, sullen the way he always was with every misjudged gift which had distinguished the marriage. She had pushed him and the dog into the kitchen away from the howling children. 'Get out,' she had said, controlling her voice with difficulty. 'You can't bloody provide for us, OK. But you don't have to make it worse. Just get out, and take that animal with you.'

Clattering up to the top deck of the bus, she remembered his slower steps, descending from the flat with an armful of smallish dog which had looked so large and hungry in their cramped living room. Remembered the hour spent placating the children in quiet fury. 'Why can't we keep it, Mum . . . why? Dad gave it us, not you . . . You're a pig, Mum . . . We'd

28

look after it, Mum ... we would really ... ' Would you hell, she muttered, promising treats in return, while it all rumbled down into quiet, solid resentment, each for the other. But even in the remembered anger, she could hear Ted's light steps going away mournfully. Always light-footed, Ted. Not known as the soft-shoed shuffler for nothing. To hell with him. But she wished she did not care what happened to him, wished she did not mind them being so ignorant of one another's lives. Didn't even know where he lived, or he where she worked. Better that way, probably. Tears threatened the bright eyeshadow and she blinked them back, staring ahead at the broad back on the seat beyond, clutching the bag on her thin knees, trying to think of food.

At ten-thirty in the morning, Sarah fled through the smoked-glass doors of the reception, noisiest person to enter and easily the latest. It was not for the golden receptionists to comment. Miss Fortune had been in a meeting since dawn, according to her secretary, and since Sarah's grin was catching and her wave towards them unrepentant as she took the stairs two at a time, the red coat rustling, her exuberance defied criticism. The other lady solicitors had been in since eight-fifteen of course, but there was something admirable in Sarah's defiant carelessness, so that, in mute conspiracy, they failed to notice the eccentricities or the appalling time-keeping, and smiled back.

The stairs led to a wide corridor, carpet still thick on the first floor, with well-tended greenery in tasteful alcoves cleverly lit against restful walls. No prints, almost spartan. On the second floor, decoration was more haphazard, the

29

corridor narrow and the ceilings lower over rooms of smaller dimensions if no less immaculate. Solid reproduction furniture to compensate for lack of size: one chair for the desk, one for a visitor and the room was almost full, would have been elegantly cramped without the mess Sarah created. Her own pictures hung on the wall to pacify her spirit and hide the feeling of being a caged bird with ruffled feathers pining for a piece of sky. Apart from these, Sarah hated it, not as much as she hated being a lawyer at all, but certainly to the same degree. This might have been prestigious Mayfair, this ghastly, pretentious, stuffy office, but on four mornings out of five, she could not raise her head from the pillow without dropping back into that sickening claustrophobia provoked by the thought of this room. A sensation of dread compounded by the certain knowledge that any other employment which used the qualifications, which felt like her own sentence for life, would be better. What a wimp she had been, what a malleable weakling, to let herself in for a lifetime of legal wrangling. Time will come, she told herself, when I shall be no one else's creature. And when I don't wake up looking for yet another reason why I should not go to work today.

As Sarah sat, applying the everyday props, face crouched to a cracked mirror in the drawer, wondering why her make-up bag always looked diseased and mascara was claggy only when she tried to apply it in a hurry, the door crashed open before Joan, a six-foot wraith bearing a large mug of coffee which was still complete with traces of yesterday's lipstick.

'Bloody hell, gel, where you been? You aren' half late.'

'Sorry. Thanks, who noticed?'

'No one much. Matthewson popped in, only for a chat, he said. Don't think he was checking up on you. Just lonely.' Matthewson was happier in these humbler regions. 'Come on then, tell me. Out late again last night, was you? Another of your deadbeats?'

'Another friend. Of the opposite sex. All right, another deadbeat, but very kind.'

'So you say. All your blokes sound useless to me.' Rich, though. Joan presupposed they were rich, Sarah's pleasant-sounding men with their secretive requests. They had rich voices! Sarah had rich clothes, richer even than all the other lady solicitors. 'You need a nice fella.' She sat down, coughed, lit another cigarette. 'Only don't marry a policeman. I'll tell you the latest when you've caught up. Ted's excelled himself.' She cackled, pushed the coffee towards Sarah, folded her arms, looked down critically. 'And do I detect just a trace of chemical poisoning?'

'Just a trace.' They had a common language. Joan considered that the chemicals in wine were solely responsible for the hangovers, and had coined a new phrase for an old condition. It looked better on a sick-note, and had confused personnel on several of hers.

'Well, gel, don't let it get to you. And in case you've gone deaf, that's your phone ringing. It's Watson and Watson. They're caving in.'

'Sarah Fortune, could you hold on a minute?' She covered the phone with one hand. 'What do you mean, caving in?'

'What do you think I bloody mean? You offered him ten thousand to settle the action last week. He was all bluff and "no, can't consider it", and this morning he's phoned three times, 'course he's caving in.' Joan strode out, thin as a stick, muttering mock despair. Panic in Sarah as she tried to remember which case, when, who were Messrs Watson and Watson, and what was the name of the client?

'Sorry to keep you. Who's speaking?'

'Mr Watson.'

'Mr Who?'

'Watson.' Roared.

'Which one? Oh yes, Mr Watson. Missed you earlier. At a meeting. Shame about that. What can I . . . '

'We accept.'

'Do you now?' Struggling with words and memory, fencing for time, with facts slipping away like eels from a net. 'Well, I'm not sure the offer stands. You refused last week. I thought again. I seem to remember my client was being generous.'

'We accept.'

'Nine thousand.'

'You said ten.'

'Then, not now. You refused then. Nine thousand, take it or leave it. I shan't ask for costs. Saves you some.'

'Wait a minute . . . '

'Haven't got a minute. Nine thousand. Just hang on a second . . . ' Stuffing the squawking phone beneath a rubble of papers, the question of which case it was tugging at bruised brain cells, wondering why she argued on automatic pilot like a compulsive bargainer when she couldn't even remember who he was or what the hell it had been about, this offer, this acceptance. Then she couldn't find the phone, and when she did, the receiver was still warm with Watson's enraged acceptance. 'Tough lady,' he said, furious but admiring. 'Don't suppose you want a job?' 'Christ,' muttered Sarah. 'That's the last thing I need.' Must be an important client for Watson, whoever he was. At times like this, ignorance was bliss. Watson could not be expected to know the difference between a hardliner and a thirty-year-old woman with a slight hangover, defective memory and no line at all.

Miss Fortune knew she was a misfit in the firm, not obviously, but subtly so, simply slightly out of focus. The firm, that big amorphous animal with all the dull instincts of a modern dinosaur, knew it without analysing why, and compromised by relegating Sarah's menage to the nether regions of the second floor so that Joan's leopard-skin tights, strident laugh and aggressive face would not alarm the clients who padded to the doors in city suits and matching briefcases. 'Here's another clone for you, Mr P,' she had once said by way of announcement to a senior partner, and after that the second floor came to suit them best. Sarah accepted Joan without a qualm, knew every foible of Joan's health, history and energetic offspring, while Joan herself would cheerfully have killed for Sarah on a good day, murdered her on the next. She held a sort of defensive, utterly suspicious affection for her employer, allowing for giggling in both their rooms with defensive sulking in-between such lassitude on Joan's behalf. She always regretted the giggles, the confidences she gave, but always gave them, grudgingly appreciative of a good boss in the full understanding that it was still a boss. With no accountant able to understand how it was that Miss Fortune made money for the firm more by luck than strictly legal judgement, no one entirely sure what she did all day, the mystification was shared by Sarah herself who did not understand it either. For half of the hours, she worked in an energetic muddle which, miraculously, generated acceptable income by inspired and soothing guesswork, bargaining and choice of barristers. For the other half she wondered how soon it would be before she was found out, planned her passage to freedom, and tried to think up new ways of shortening her day. A talent for guarding other people's money from litigious predators ensured survival, but nothing altered the fact that she loathed it. How could anyone in their right mind be interested in the Law? People counted, not the rules. The Law is an ass, but around Sarah, it brayed with enthusiasm.

There was a short interval of silence in Sarah's room while she looked at the mess of papers made worse by the scrabble for the phone. Then came a slight knock at the door, the diffident tap of someone who had evaded the eagle eye behind the outer desk.

'Come in, Fred.' It was a conspiratorial whisper. He hovered in the doorway, a down-at-heel caretaker, sloppy to the toe nails. Fred wore the same shirt most days. His braces were frayed and his eyes permanently bloodshot. The grin on his face showed pure affection and slight mental sub-normality.

Fred was permanently shunned, smelt of fish and the boiler room, even though there was no boiler room.

''Ere, Miss Fortune. Brought your bacon roll.'

'Thanks, Fred. I need it.' She fumbled in her purse, exchanging cash for the paper bag he held out like a precious gift, thankful and grateful for the very sight of his lopsided, sheepish grin. She grinned back, her face split in open welcome. They were friends, possibly the only allies under this competitive roof. The bacon roll lay there, comfortably greasy on her desk, cholesterol fix for the day. Fred, who had already eaten two, sat down and pulled out his cigarettes. Fred's fags were legendary. They smelt too. Sarah had simply never noticed, and ate the roll with the delicacy of a hungry red squirrel, talking between bites. 'Come on then, Fred,' she said. 'What's the news?'

He shuffled happily. 'Well, not much, see? But our Ernest has got the grumps. Going round like a bear with a sore head. Reckon the missus feeds him too much. Bad tempered as hell, couldn't cheer him up.'

'What, not even with a bacon roll from the corner?'

'Nope. Nothing doing. Go away, Fred, he said to me, bugger off. So I thought I'd give you today's tip instead. Couldn't get Ernest to listen. Usually does, though.'

'What tip's this then, Fred?'

He leant forward. 'Horse called Pink Jade in the two-thirty at Epsom. Bloke in the café really rates it. Says it'll go like a bomb, nothing to stop it. Knows a bookie. Got something on it himself. What do you reckon?'

'Two pounds each way?'

'Fiver to win? Be a devil.'

'Go on then. I'll have your guts for garters if it doesn't.'

The grin grew wider, dividing his face into two triangles as he shuffled to his feet.

'Sure as eggs is eggs. Tell you what, Miss F, how about putting something on for Mr Matthewson? Might change his mood if he wins.'

'OK. Two pounds each way for him. How's my account? Do I owe you any?'

'Naa. We're looking pretty good. You're always in credit, never let me down. See you then, better get to work.'

'Watch out for Joan. She's got the hump too.'

'What's different?' They shared the look of plotters and a mutual shrug without malice before the door closed behind him.

The morning was filled with little incentive schemes. Lunch was booked, and that could be stretched to two hours. Nevertheless, Sarah sat idly. Outside in the street, tyres squealed; there was a sound of impact. She shut her eyes, stung by the sudden memory, and did not move to look.

When Sarah Fortune's handsome husband had relinquished his uninsured life nearly three years before in a car crash of resounding stupidity, he had not been entirely sober, and was talking as fast as usual. Crossing a red light in fourth gear whilst engrossed in the business of discussing a better hotel room for the next assignation, resulted in the tidy compression of his chest, a bloodless crushing; no evidence on his face, so that his companion, protected by the seat-belt he had ignored, tried to shake him awake before the police arrived. It had complicated life for Sarah to discover that the companion in question was her own sister, who spilled the beans of this incestuous attachment at the same time as her stricken face imparted the news of death. Sarah's family had never been supportive – she knew them already for the tribe of treacherous bullies they were – but all the same she agreed to Jeannie's immediate request to keep this liaison with Sarah's husband secret from Jeannie's own. She remembered asking repeatedly, what about the people in the other car? Were they hurt, tell me, were they hurt? No revenge adding to the wreckage, but in retrospect, remembering herself agreeing with Jeannie a story for public consumption, Sarah wondered at herself. Extraordinary what one person will ask of another, and what the other will agree to do.

No one had known, except a fat man called Malcolm (who had a way with children and other bodies), met at a party two years before. In the middle of the night she had told him and he had seemed to know what she meant. All sorts of other things she had told him too, even about the baby. Funny what she had done then, in a passion of liking. Funnier what she had done since. She had even told Malcolm about school, making him laugh in the early hours. 'Brains,' said her teacher, 'bring res-pons-ib-ility ... do-you-understand?' Adding one more thwack with each syllable for the rude message on the blackboard. 'And the word cop-ul-ation is spelt with one P, don't you know?' Sarah knew, but it was someone else who had written. Her own childish behaviour was then as good as her childish spelling, but life had the effect of shedding one moral principle a year and leaving a greater desire for fun than there had ever been for obedience. She had never told anyone else, apart from the same fat man, about the baby. Dead child of faithless spouse who had impregnated a sister as well as a wife, and left his debts instead of the result. Three months' life oozing away six weeks after his, drenching another car seat, while somehow, in that red, embarrassing flow, there had slid from her the whole code by which she had thought to have lived. I loved you once. You blocked my view of the universe once, both of you, but I cannot lie down and die. Nothing as insubstantial as fidelity, duty, honour or the dignity of hard work seemed faintly significant after that, nor had these old inhibitions recovered ever since. There was no place for them. Kindness, yes. Honesty of her own peculiar kind, but not the rest. Sarah stretched in her seat, one limb at a time, smiled into the distance, then chuckled out loud. On the whole, apart from the work and the grief, it had been a bloody good two years.

She dictated letters, vaguely hoping that none of the stuffy partners downstairs would ever have cause to read them.

'Dear Mr Jones ... Sorry about the size of this bill, but I did warn you Mr Justice Harvey is a mean old demon, and you were likely to lose ... Better luck next time ... Please pay us soon, we know you can afford it ...'

The door thumped against the visitor's chair, adding another chip to the mahogany veneer. Behind was a vision in fake fur with the bright blonde wisps of dyed hair half-tucked into an orange toque. It was eleven-forty-five. 'Just off to lunch,' said Joan, defying her to look at the clock. Sarah did not look. 'That time already? Thank heaven. See you later.' No rebuke, not even a mild one. Both knew better than to specify how much later.

Freedom for at least an hour, secured by striding across the foyer as if *en route* to yet another meeting. Charles Tysall sat waiting for Ernest Matthewson, who was delaying upstairs, dreading the encounter. Charles was hidden behind one of the huge ferns Ernest so loathed, following Sarah's exit with puzzled eyes, half-rising from his seat in the desire to run after the mane of red hair, sitting back instead, with alarm and relief moving across his closed face. He would have Sarah Fortune. He was determined to let her refuse as much as she liked, but for now he needed to talk.

Plodding downstairs, Ernest felt his head begin to throb. Charles Tysall had him by the balls, and there was no one to tell. Although the firm did not handle more than half of Tysall's monetary affairs (luckily, they were spared the shadiest), they still needed him. As Ernest put it to himself, they needed the loss of Tysall as a client like they needed a hole in the head, and if they lost work generated by him, they would lose half the income of the practice.

Therefore, he had to be pleased, and he knew he had to be favoured, which meant long lunches with Charles, and even longer confessions. Halfway downstairs, Ernest looked at the pale walls, saw the same tasteful colours he had seen in Tysall's house, somehow spattered with blood. He had tried to make Charles seek help, in the bumbling way Ernest did everything: 'Really, old man, it's a bit much, shouldn't you ...' 'Shouldn't I what?' Charles would say, looking at him over the rim of a glass, smiling at his helplessness. 'Shouldn't I what? What do you mean?' Ernest had failed, conspicuously; he had known the man, and had never once liked him. Ernest had never before found a client he could not like for something, even if it were nothing more than the imagination of his dishonesty, but he had never anticipated one quite so brutal. But he knew equally well, from the oldest school of solicitors, from practices taught him by his father and grandfather, that he should never reveal what he was told, should be utterly bound by his client's confidence. Whatever the value of the belief, he could not relinquish it now, and Tysall was fully aware of that reliability. Ernest could only hope the mere act of talking might curtail some of the excesses.

Damn him. Damn him. How long since, oh, more than a year or two, when Ernest had asked that standard question, 'How's the wife, Charles?' Receiving the cold reply, 'Dead, I think.' Ernest had choked, and in the midst of the choking, listened.

'I tried to kill her. No, not really, but she was so very unfaithful, you see ...'

Ernest did not see. He envisaged his wife, who had always been unfaithful to her own son in her way, he could see that, but never, ever to him. He listened to Charles proceeding, matter-of-fact, unhurried, the calm, handsome face not even flustered.

'She was not in any kind of order. Unfaithful, according to the evidence. So I had to cut her face, to teach her a lesson.'

40

'Had to?' murmured Ernest, remembering the wonderful Titian beauty of the woman, a bit like Sarah Fortune when he came to think of it.

'Had to? Surely not?'

'Yes, it was necessary. Women have to be punished.'

'I see,' said Ernest, and continued eating with his soul disturbed, each mouthful like cardboard. 'I see.' What a mistake, he sometimes reflected, to even pretend you understand, especially when you do not comprehend at all.

In the face of his silence, there had followed an account of the first attempt by Charles to strangle his wife, recited while delicate food expanded in Ernest's mouth, sticking in his throat. Then there had been more, the history of all the episodes since, the memory of all those cool anecdotes of horror. I cannot tell, Ernest told himself in a daily litany. I cannot ever tell. What is told to me in confidence, I cannot ever tell. So his father had said, God knows what he had heard: trust is a sacred privilege, as well as a curse. Beware of it. Ernest had armed himself, but he did not know what to do. Without a God to whom he should pray, he simply did nothing.

But he worried about the women. Whoever they were, escaping with their lives, they never complained. Charles Tysall was too powerful for that. Ernest knew it all, understood not a jot. Hoped against hope Tysall would never find a passion so grand it could merit the ultimate finale, some final, insane revenge from an insane mind. Even Ernest knew he was dealing with a madman of enormous civility. It made him fear him more.

Secrecy. All in the lawyers' code, a kind of vow, till death do us part. Ernest missed his son, for the jokes and the games and the telling of secrets, and, thinking of Malcolm as a kind of talisman, reached the foyer as Sarah Fortune left it, smiled at Charles, and gritted his teeth. To listen without forgiveness, to hear without an element of understanding, to endure his confidences in an endless, sickening silence, full of fear.

CHAPTER THREE

Malcolm did not understand his own persistence. Forgetting the occasional triumphs, at this single moment in time he shared Ernest's incomprehension as to why any man should take his considerable legal talents to the grubby back-streets of prosecuting crime. A life of litigation for the rich seemed infinitely preferable.

With one accord, he and Detective Sergeant Ryan had stopped by the railings and looked down. Neither wanted to move, both of them were utterly depressed. They might have parted at the door of Counsel's chambers, each to nurture, or drown, his own disappointment, but they had not parted, they stuck together in grim silence until they reached Temple Lawns, rounded the corner into a colourful sun. After nine years of it, Malcolm had tutored himself beyond the kind of impotent fury he used to feel when the guilty celebrated acquittal. Having resolved that these travesties would not be the result of poor prosecutions, shoddy paperwork and indifferent investigation, he tried to shrug his shoulders. Even so, trudging away from the chambers of Simeon Churcher QC, he had felt the weight of frustration like a sack on his shoulders, heavier than the papers in the bag. Not even an acquittal; more a question of horse falls at first gate due to sabotage. It was inevitable, he was accustomed to it, but never in a hundred years would Ryan relinquish the bitter disappointment, and Malcolm felt all the worse for that.

They had walked from King's Bench Walk, adapting their steps to one another as if handcuffed, Ryan had thought, but reluctant to part. Through Pump Court, silent still at four-thirty, early yet for the rush of after-court footsteps. Through the archway across Middle Temple Lane and into Fountain Court with pretty summer shadows and elegant fountain. Of all the facts of his professional life which Malcolm was able to absorb with such ease, the sheer prettiness of the Temple, its clubbish discretion, cobble stones and gracious buildings, filled him with wonder. Inside these well-proportioned windows, premium space was broken down into small rooms where disrobed barristers of various means and abilities sat with murderers, fraudsmen, uncomfortable policemen and defrocked bankers, distressed wives and violent husbands, giving unacceptable advice in calm tones. 'You must plead guilty, Mr X. Don't worry, you'll only get five years,' and yet no one ranted and screamed in this place, or even broke a window. Above, or below it all, the ladies and gentlemen of the Bar sailed out to play, leaving mayhem behind them.

Down on the brilliant green of Inner Temple Lawns, waitresses with black dresses and white pinafores were loading snowy tables. Glistening canapés appeared on plates, ice buckets stood to attention filled with unpopped bottles. Ryan licked his lips, and turned to Malcolm.

'What these buggers celebrating, then?'

'Being alive, I suppose. It's an annual event. One of several. Middle Temple Garden Party. Most of the Inns of Court have something like this. Then there's the Inner Temple May Ball, the Christmas cocktails, indoors, of course; Gray's Inn Ball, grandest of the lot. They like to enjoy themselves.'

'So I see.' The Detective Sergeant sighed, watching the activity, curious rather than envious. He preferred pubs, champagne made him sick. No, it wasn't champagne, it was weddings, the only time he encountered fizzy drinks, which made him sick.

'So that's why old Churcher made it a short conference. He had to rush off and polish his tie. Dry old stick, isn't he?' Malcolm sighed, hearing the sharp edge of Ryan's resentment.

'We wouldn't have liked him whether he was dry, wet or middling.' Ryan made a sound between a sigh and a snore. 'Bailey told me this would happen.'

From behind them came puffing and rattling. A red-faced boy stepped inside the gate to the gardens, deposited a crate of champagne and a box of glasses with a dangerous thump, then ran across the lawns for instructions. Ryan looked at the crate, and Malcolm looked away. Ryan opened his huge briefcase, and reaching deftly for one bottle of the champagne and two flute glasses, placed them neatly inside the case with a wodge of papers between them. Without a word, the two men moved down the steps towards the Embankment.

'I reckon,' Ryan sighed again, 'since I hate barristers and this little lot gets paid out of Legal Aid and such, while I just pay my taxes, they owe me, not the other way round, and they didn't ask us to their party. How about a seat by the river, Mr Cook?'

In the end, they leant on the pigeon-stained wall, watching the movement of the sluggish low-tide river. 'You do the honours, Mr Cook. Makes you an aider and abettor to theft, you know, and all you lot ought to try it once or twice. Besides, you'll be more used to champagne corks than me. I don't go to many garden parties if you see what I mean. Only weddings.'

The first glass had its reviving effect. Ryan noticed how Malcolm preserved the posture of the fat man, distanced himself even as he smiled, giving himself space even as he slumped. Ryan took out a cigarette, passed the packet to Malcolm, lit his own and inhaled with the deep satisfaction of an addict.

'Can't even bloody smoke in Churcher's chambers. What a pillock. What the hell does he do down the cells with a client on Monday morning?'

'He doesn't go down the cells with prisoners on Monday mornings. He's not that kind of barrister, doesn't do much crime, if any. Company and Commercial, all that stuff; that's what he does. Real money. That's why I used him. We needed a Silk with the know-how to sift through a mile of documents. To tell the truth, I never thought we'd have much joy on the theft side, but I hoped we might find something in Tysall's bloody records which would give us a clue where to go next. Some other way to get a crack at him.'

'Clever bastard.' The Detective Sergeant drained the glass, looked round him with a grin, pulled the bottle from behind the briefcase.

'Same again, sir?'

'Don't mind if I do ...'

'This would be nicer with cheese and onion crisps,' said Ryan.

Both sipped, temporarily content.

'Mind you,' Ryan continued, replacing the bottle, 'old Churcher has a way with words. At least he'd read the papers. Good of him.'

'And let us know he'd done his homework. Good customer relations, only he won't want many customers like us. Not on what the Crown Prosecution Service pays him. He'd rehearsed it. This is the case, as I see it, Mr Cook. Mr Ryan ... Pay attention, boys ...' Malcolm mimicked Churcher's clipped tones. 'We have Mr Tysall, our putative co-defendant, who owns several companies. One of these is dealing in er ... new technology. Produces not very exciting er ... packages, needs new ideas. He spots a smaller company consisting of a little team of brilliant graduates who've formulated a revolutionary new piece of software which, when harnessed, will put this struggling outfit on the billion-dollar map. They've devoted three years and all their capital to research. However, not all of them are otherworldly boffins.

By dint of seduction of one young graduate, female, you'll be glad to know at least, and another young man in Company A's team, our Tysall persuades them to come and work for him, at exorbitant salaries. Provided of course they bring the er . . . package with them.'

'Giftwrapped for preference.'

'Which it was. The defectors do not tell Company A, of course. Who do not know until market rumours tell them that Tysall's lot are launching a revolution sooner and better marketed than their own could ever be. Altered, of course, for cosmetic reasons, but still the same. Only we have to prove it's the same. Prove that the defectors have not created something out of their egg-shaped heads, but have actually stolen er . . . data, discs, whole programmes and ideas, solicited by our Mr Tysall. So, Mr Cook, Mr Ryan, you find a computer expert who says, for several hundred pounds a day, he will make a detailed comparison to show how this must be the case. There are few experts in this field, they are vastly expensive and all as incomprehensible as one another. The jury will not understand, Mr Cook, Mr Ryan. What is more, they will listen to three weeks' gobbledy-gook, and they will not care. It is not theft as they know it, it is employees squabbling, it is only money and computers. Even if a small firm faces bankruptcy and a rich one stands to gain revenue of ten million. Meantime, our expert and myself have bored them to death at vast public expense for a result we cannot guarantee. This is not, Mr Cook, Mr Ryan, a gamble I advise. Send Company A to the High Court to pursue his civil remedies . . .'

'. . . And you told him the complainant Company couldn't afford to do that, that's why he's come to the police. He don't want damages, he wants his programme, and is now on the brink of shooting himself. Remember what Churcher said?'

'Yes, I do. He took his glasses off, and said, "That is very sad, Mr Cook. I hope you advise him against it. Not a course I recommend." I mean, how would he know?'

Both men collapsed against the wall, snuffling with unexplained giggles. Again Ryan caught himself in surprise. Even in the midst of uncontrolled laughter, he expected Malcolm to be fat. It was odd to see the thinner man chuckle and explode as the fat one had done. Thank God some things don't change, thought Ryan, wiping his eyes, reaching for the bottle. 'He's not a bad old stick, Churcher,' he said, gasping. 'He just doesn't appreciate what it's going to be like telling this Young Turk we aren't going to prosecute and his company is going down the pan. But he did understand the difficulties, some of them. What was it he said? I know. "These days, Mr Ryan, we rarely have the means to prosecute fraud, or even complicated theft. You have my sympathy. Being in the Fraud Squad must be similar to riding a horse and cart in pursuit of a Porsche."'

'He's right, of course,' said Malcolm. 'He was right about everything. What sticks in my gullet is the fact that if it were a man on the factory floor, stealing bits from cars, or computers for that matter, only computer bits aren't useful, he'd be charged and put inside. Just because it's complicated ideas being pinched for a loss and profit worth millions, Tysall gets away scot-free. For the third bloody time, the third stolen company, on almost identical facts. All those ruined lives.'

'To them that hath it shall be given. The water always flows into the valley. Didn't know I went to church, did you, Mr Cook?'

'No,' said Malcolm. 'I didn't, and I wouldn't have guessed.' Both immediately dissolved again. Malcolm fell against the wall, stood upright, braced himself. 'Right. Shame. There's a good pub in Fleet Street; should be open by now. Time for a swift half? Between wives?'

'Not like you, Mr Cook, not these days.' Ryan shook his head. 'Can't get used to you being so careful, Mr Cook, I really can't. I'm pleased you still drink. I been worried about you. Still a big man, though. Room for a pint.'

'Sometimes. In good company I return to my old habits. Not often.'

They ambled past the Inner Temple Lawns. 'Shall I put back the glasses, do you think?' Ryan asked.

'I don't think so,' said Malcolm. 'Don't tempt fate.'

'But I'm an officer of the law.'

'And I, a solicitor of the Supreme Court. A serving member of the Crown Prosecution Service, aiding and abetting a police officer to steal champagne. The average judge would have a lot of sympathy, but what would you do if you were drummed out, Ryan?'

Ryan grinned. 'Become a pimp, or a private detective. Like Ted Plumb. Did you ever know him? Rochester Row?'

'No.'

'Lately of the Drugs Squad. Good copper once. Drummed

out. Now all the things I've just mentioned, pimp, detective, bouncer. Works for Charles Tysall, I hear, but wouldn't talk to me. I did try.'

'Well, if you got the sack, Charles Tysall would give you a job.'

'Would he hell. Don't put me in the same bracket as Ted Plumb. I have my pride. I'd rather be a publican. That would suit me better.'

'Well, watch it, Ryan, will you?' said Malcolm lightly. 'Don't ever expect too much by way of results. It's disappointment makes policemen bent. When they cease to see the point of playing by the rules. If you see what I mean.'

'Yes,' said Ryan, just as lightly. 'I do see, as it happens.'

The lawns were filling. Black suits, wives with peacock hats, dark-suited ladies straight out of court, discreetly painted faces with just a hint of a frivolous frill at the neck, colourful against the green and the hats and the old young heads. Only Ryan paused to look back after they had passed the same steps, suddenly, vainly anxious for the boy who would have to account for the bottle.

'Hey! Mr Cook! I've just seen bloody Churcher talking to a lovely redhead, crafty old bugger. No wonder he wanted rid of us.'

'Good luck to him,' said Malcolm. 'I hear he's a widower. Whoever he talks to isn't even scandalous. Maybe she'll soften him up before we ever have to see him again.'

'Widower? Single man? All right for some. Not a bad old bloke really. Oh, come on, Mr Cook. If we're going to drink, let's drink. And not in bloody Fleet Street. I need a beer . . .'

*

Looking at his own haphazard reflection, Simeon Churcher was aware of something wrong but what it was escaped him. Like why it was the business of his day was so easy if complicated, while the business of his evenings was so awful. All his life he had been setting himself goals, achieving them more or less with the kind of precision useful to Queen's Counsel engrossed in commercial litigation, but these days nothing came naturally at all, while the mirror showed signs of the now familiar panic and Simeon was forced to recognise in his own lopsidedness not only how useless he was without a wife, but what a hash he was making of finding a replacement.

The incident of her death was remote now, like an old, but well remembered case. Mrs Churcher had usually been ill, but well enough to run her household with an iron hand, frequently discarding any velvet glove. The end result was Simeon in pressed socks and pristine appearance to compensate for years of virtual celibacy and incessant headaches, with his innocence preserved by twice-daily telephone calls to his clerk in order to plot his movements and nourishment as would a general for his army. Pleased to be the subject of such concern, he had never rebelled; but now when he strode down Fleet Street towards the High Court he kept his eyes fixed on the ground to avoid the distraction of what they might otherwise observe, bumping into short skirts with groans of dismay, Simeon was as hungry for an affectionate sexual encounter as he had been at sixteen, with a level of ignorance almost as complete. Two problems compounded by fifty-four years of total respectability. Simeon yearned for adventures with a kindly, instructive mate, and from the depths of his imagination, the new wife rose a phoenix from the ashes, while all the time there was something in his approach which sent all prospects scuttling for cover like hysterical ants in the path of his large feet. They did not walk away. They ran.

'Jesus.' Joan was speaking to Sarah. 'That was that Simeon Churcher. Again. Why didn't you see the danger signs with him, Sarah? He's rung for you three times today. It's like listening to a man fall over himself on the phone. You must've bowled him over at that posh garden party you was on about.'

'My heels were stuck in the grass. I was shrinking by inches, I couldn't move. Besides, he's a nice man. He's taking me out to dinner.'

'He's bloody what? You must be mad, and why do you go for such losers? You won't bloody go out with Charles Tysall, best-looking bloke who ever crossed this sodding doorstep, rich, handsome, gorgeous . . .'

'I did. Go out with him. Once or twice was enough, and anyway I thought we agreed we wouldn't discuss it.'

'Sorry, I'm sure. Won't mention it again. Was it because he was a client?' You poor cow, she thought.

'No. Besides, he isn't a client. Not one of mine. I only saw him because Ernest was out. Charles Tysall has problems beyond my slender skills.'

'Well, it ain't for me to comment, but you must have a screw loose. Bloody good-looking bloke. And rich. Wouldn't catch me missing a chance like that.'

Sarah stirred, fidgeted. She's all right, thought Joan. I like her really, and I bloody well owe her plenty, but it doesn't do any harm for her to worry from time to time. Nice to see it. Makes her human.

'I'm a bit frightened of him, to tell the truth.'

Joan snorted, and hoisted the files from the desk and under her arm. 'Never known you frightened of anything, Miss Fortune. Not you.'

Simeon considered he was looking rather pukka. As far as he was able to judge. He was a slight man, with grizzled, grey hair, bright eyes, a large mouth and hands which he used for copious gestures in court and could not otherwise keep still. The appearance in the mirror still worried him. Today he wore cavalry twills, and an ancient bluey tweed jacket devoid of shape and unpleasantly hairy, slightly at odds with his nylon shirt of brilliant yellowy-white and a half-purple, striped tie, saddened and twisted in the wash. His new shoes shone like plastic. The combined effect diminished and aged him into a retired colonel, without batman, and if he had wished to complete the general impression of dated ineptitude, Simeon could rely on his manner to do the rest. Excellent choice, the Travellers' Club. Pall Mall's faded splendour. It had been himself at fault, and he knew it, crestfallen when she said she had been there before, but how grand it was. Grinning like a pixie he had been when she had found him too early in the entrance, bestowing his smiles indiscriminately on all passers-by in case they were her, hopelessly surprised to find that this warm lady, met so opportunely on the Inner Temple Lawns, would actually arrive. Sarah Fortune had no sharp edges to distract from her neat and confident elegance and transparent intelligence. He did not understand women's clothes, but the combination of sexiness with complete respectability unhinged him completely. There was the ready laughter in her throat, so lacking in contempt, an understanding in the smile, and despite his twitching, he sank into a state bordering on calm.

Dinner had passed with relative ease, apart from his realisation that he had placed her facing the wall with the token vase of carnations between them, so that he gabbled and she questioned with both of them peering between the leaves. At one stage she had moved it to one side, and he had replaced it nervously without knowing he did so. The hands. He could never control the hands. New shoes were hurting as he tripped on the way down the staircase into the library, crushing her briefly against the banister, but she did not seem to mind. All going well, only three or four gaffes. If Miss Fortune had counted rather more than that, she did not say.

Too successful, of course. Simeon had relaxed too soon. As she lit a cigarette to accompany coffee, an automatic gesture on her part, his own reaction was spontaneous. Smoking had been anathema to Mrs Churcher, forbidden in her house: no smoke, no nicotine, all rooms immediately freshened, and Simeon had copied her set response. As the first curl of smoke trailed from Sarah's cigarette, he automatically produced a large red handkerchief from his bulging pockets and flicked it absently but loudly in front of him. Among the subdued murmurings of the library, the gesture was flamboyant, certainly clumsy. The edge of the cloth caught the cigarette in the ashtray, sent it flying on to the carpet before the second flick caught the coffee cup she had extended to him. Liquid and cup rose in the air for a brief and graceful moment, then crashed against the table as a huge brown stain appeared on Sarah's skirt.

'Sorry,' said Simeon, his voice manically loud and cheerful even in his own ears. 'My wife hated cigarette smoke.'

The girl's face was looking at him strangely, twisted slightly in a kind of grimace, reminding him, surely not, of someone attempting not to cry. 'Ah,' she said quietly. 'I suppose that explains it. Will you excuse me a minute?'

She was off like a shot, out of the long room almost at a run, leaving him to breathe heavily, rumple the handkerchief and wonder at his own offence. Down in the basement Ladies, Sarah Fortune relinquished stern control of her face, and collapsed in helpless laughter. He needed help. Carefully she wiped her eyes and repaired the damage.

But alone in the library, subjected to a few curious glances, Simeon was suddenly, blindingly aware of what he had done. People did not deserve to be abused, swatted like flies and covered in hot coffee for the simple antisocial crime of lighting a cigarette. They didn't deserve it; some people liked cigarettes, judging from those around him, many people. He might have been competent to advise on the devious shameful Mr Charles Tysalls of the world, but otherwise, his ignorance was profound. Being clever, he realised, was a hindrance.

Simeon prepared to leave, stiff with embarrassment. He did not blame her for not coming back, could see no reason why she should.

Two light hands were on his shoulders, and her face, curtained by sleek red hair, was bending towards his own, her eyes alight with amusement.

'Do you think I could have that coffee now, from the cup?'

For that deft touch of forgiveness, Simeon could have given her the world. They had managed to speak as if nothing had happened, as if his pockets were not bulging with boy scout detritus and three handkerchieves, and parted, friendly and reserved. In that little absence she had somehow assumed charge, and given him hope.

Words were difficult. Two days later, Sarah reviewed the evening with Simeon and sighed. One task then, before forgetting all others. She had picked up the telephone with something akin to trepidation, telling herself it did not matter. These were the episodes she most disliked.

'Simeon?'

'Sarah? I'm delighted you rang. How are you?'

'Better for hearing you. Now, my dear, what do you think about another meeting?'

No foolish girlish promptings. No clues. No pretending that the circumstances of their meeting had been entirely ordinary or the evening perfect.

'I think about it all the time,' he stammered. 'You know I do, and how much . . . But it won't do, and I won't do for you, if you know what I mean . . . I want to, but can't.' That understanding teasing voice of hers, he could feel himself melting.

'Well.'

Strange how he knew what she was going to say before she said it, not the words, but simply the meaning wrapped in a great and sensitive generosity. And did not mind in the least.

'You aren't the answer to a maiden's prayer, any more than I'm a maiden, you know.' Gently said. 'You want a wife, and don't know how to court one. I don't want a husband, as it happens, but I like you well enough. Would you like it if we were to meet from time to time? Until the maiden answers the prayer? To make you fitter for her? You aren't at the moment, you know, but you don't need me to tell you that.'

'No I don't. And I agree. I'd love to see you.'

'Dinner next week, then. Or a play. Or an evening in.'

'All three,' he said earnestly. 'If you don't mind.'

She laughed, and his fists uncurled at the sound of it. A happy laugh she had, as comforting as a hug and as full of promise.

'One problem,' he began.

'Which is?' From the first, he loved her mild, questioning voice.

'What if we don't get on?'

'What do you mean?' Not defensive, simply an insistence that he, rather than herself, should express any reservation.

'Supposing we don't accord, I mean, I'm not much used to . . .' He stopped in confusion.

'Oh, I wouldn't worry about that. We'll be fine.'

Such an airy confidence. He believed in her, felt the burden of inadequacy fall from his stooped shoulders like a pack.

'Are you sure?'

'Of course. I'll have to look after you if not.' Again that laughter, entirely free of scorn or condescension. 'Next week? Wait a minute, I'll get my diary . . .'

Sarah stretched very shapely limbs on a pretty sofa, sank into her glass of wine in a quick survey of a favourite comfortable room and the prospect of hours of silence. Oh, for a short life and a merry one, but look at the mess. It was not the larger, moral issues which ever troubled her conscience, not any more. They were shrunk into minor dilemmas the way she considered sensible, second to all the endless problems of how to keep the house clean, manage shopping for necessities, and hold all the thin threads which made life possible. She had run out of washing-up liquid again, there was always that irritating pile of cups on the draining-board, clothes to be mended or cleaned. She had avoided the corner shop on the way home, guiltily evading the sad gaze of the lady behind the counter and the thirtieth chapter of her life waiting to be told as the twenty-ninth had been told that morning. Sarah always listened, but sometimes it was harder than others. The fridge contained one egg, a piece of venerable cheese, two onions and a bottle of oil. Difficult to make a feast out of that. She had the depressing suspicion her bedroom was a mess, remembering the tights flung on the floor that morning in the frantic search for a pair with both legs, to say nothing of the earrings, tipped and spilt in the usual hurried search for one to match another. Such sophistication you have, Sarah. What a joke, what a glorious muddle. Home. No food, nor ironed shirts for the morning, place needing a dust. She looked at it from the safety of the

59

horizontal, squinted at the untidiness, saw the box containing new shoes and a sideways view of a favourite painting alongside an open bottle of wine. What the hell. All right, there was an hour or two of chores, then she would be able to sing in the bath while washing away the day, before going out to look at the world again. A night world, different and better balm for restlessness.

Sarah moved with energy, crossing the hall by the mirror, into her bedroom, waving at the glass dismissively. Don't ever look in the mirror, she had warned herself, for signs of what life does to you. You chose it, you can always opt out, but don't damn well pity it. Don't look. You only ever grow old and ugly by surrounding yourself with malice. And discontent. And that office. You only stay sane by doing exactly as you please as nearly as you can, with as much honesty as time allows. Which is what I think I do. Too many years of doing the opposite, being good for nothing else but being good, whilst being good to no one.

The kitchen depressed her as usual. Maybe one day she would have somewhere in a wilderness with all the total independence she craved, free from the dual tyrannies of mortgage and employment. Maybe she would borrow some children, paint pictures, live without a bloody answerphone. She played back the messages on her own, absently dusting the table on which it stood. All lawyers, all business. 'Hallo, Sarah. How about lunch next week?' (She must remember to take the book he had wanted.) Another. ' . . . Just phoning to say thanks for conference the other afternoon. When next? Soon, I hope. Please phone.' Measured English tones: John's voice, Judge Henry's voice, Albemarle *et al*. No, thought Sarah. I mean, yes. Yes I will have another glass of wine. Cottage in the country, room in a lighthouse. Yes. But not yet, not for a while. I like this secrecy, I like this life.

And today my horse won. Pink Jade again, backed by Fred. Not bad for a girl.

Chapter Four

'How long have you been in the police, Mr Ryan?'

'Oh Christ. Since I was born.'

'No, I can't put that. Perhaps that's just what it feels like . . .'

'Thirteen years, then.'

'Lucky for some. Any substantiated complaints?'

'No, not yet. There've been some unsubstantiated.'

'Never mind. Those don't count. Any commendations, Commissioners' or judges'?'

'One.'

'Married? Children? Sorry to ask, but we have to know for the witness statement.'

'Yes to both.' And sod off if you want to ask anything else. He was sick of it. Two interviews in one week, one with CIB, MS14 or whatever the hell it was those maniacs investigating complaints against police officers called themselves these days. All because that bastard Tysall had (a) made a formal complaint about the seizing of documents from the offices of his computer company, even though they had all been returned, and (b) followed it up with a High Court writ against the Commissioner for damages. First, the interview by that faceless Scot with the obsessive gleam in his eye and the plain-clothes demeanour of a crafty thug, but at least a policeman, and then this friendlier chat with an equally faceless solicitor from the Commissioner's small fleet. All had been explained. 'The Commissioner is liable for the acts of his constables, by law. He is sued a few hundred times every year.' 'Oh yeah?' Ryan had joked. 'That's worse than the gas board. Now who would want to work for a man like that?'

Malicious, tight-fisted bastard. Tysall could spot money under a stone, and if he fell into his own cesspit, he'd come up smelling of roses. That's what Eton and Oxford does for you. Solicitors' department was airless, slotted into an ugly block along with Catering, Medical and Surveyors above a foyer smelling of onions from the traffic wardens' canteen in the basement. The complaints office was aptly placed in a building resembling Alcatraz on the south side of the river. Ryan almost missed his smaller, colder office in the Fraud Squad, and for a moment thought of it with affection.

'Listen, sir. Me and Fraud, we're incompatible, that's what.' So he had told Superintendent Bailey who had pinched him from District. 'I'm not too good at reading and writing, sir,' he had finished lamely. 'Too bad,' Bailey had said. 'You need the promotion and your wife needs the regular hours.'

Stitched up good and proper, and to start with he could feel the thread cutting into his skin.

Paperwork forever, he thought. No street pounding, no pubs, no chases, no great gulps of outrage, only money. But that was before Tysall, before Ryan understood how he should have trusted Bailey after all. Fraud wasn't so bland, not once he cottoned on to how Bailey had got him on the squad to get his teeth into Tysall. There was a roomful of Tysall, and Ryan hated Tysall with a passion. Exactly as Bailey had intended.

Back in the chilly confines of his room in Holborn, Ryan rekindled the flames, forgot the humiliating interviews. On his desk, read briefly before he had left, was a slender report from District, slimline through lack of effort and a dearth of questions.

'Diana Steepel. D.o.b. 18.10.1960. 13a, Olympia Mansions, West Kensington. Suicide Report.

'On Tues, 15th August 1988, Ms Steepel was found by her neighbour who had forced the door of the flat to investigate a dripping tap. Subject had taken an overdose of sleeping tablets, plus large quantity of gin. One half-bottle remained. The flatmate does not drink, and was away for a fortnight's holiday.

'It is apparent Ms Steepel intended suicide. The pathologist says that the attempt would not have been successful through a combination of alcohol and Mogadon if the victim had not woken, probably nauseous, but unable through weakness to vomit effectively, and without any help at hand. Cause of death: asphixiation. No note, but victim known to have been severely depressed. No signs of violence or disturbance ... '

Perhaps a cry for help? Perhaps, but not likely. Ryan closed the file in disgust. Pleas for help were made with the clear prospect of rescue, and she'd deliberately chosen the time when her flatmate was away. She had not been seeking deliverance, Tysall's brilliant graduate, who had defected to his ranks with all her brain cells intact, but not the rest of her, apparently. Tysall lived less than a mile away, in a straight line. She'd probably moved to be nearer him, then been abandoned, poor cow. Probably wanted to sleep for ever. He'd had the body and used up the brain. At least Annie, pretty and plump, love of Ryan's own life, rebounding from him to be seduced by Tysall, was still alive. Back in her own home town, silent, only mentally scarred. Ready to marry the nearest worzel farmer if she hadn't done it already. Anything to remove the mortal sins of two seductions and one abortion.

At least I loved Annie. That bastard never loved anyone. Annie loved me too. Guilt surfaced in his mind, a kind of sudden heartburn distilled into fury and pain.

Ryan marshalled all his reports on Tysall, including the last in a varied and tragic line. Three or four bankrupt companies, and Steepel, bankrupt life, pretty kid. Just as well Bailey encouraged Ryan's empirical style of investigation and turned a blind eye to it. In the face of Bailey's Nelsonian telescope, Ryan worked by instinct, found himself a bad man rather than a good suspicion. Tysall had emerged into woozy focus from all the rumour-mongering, tales told by disassociated witnesses and informants, information

65

leaking from other investigations. The Fraud teams worked like that, names falling off carousels or found in the bran-tub with irksome regularity. From all this dross, company frauds, bent mortgage applications, other men's double lives and sticky fingers, Tysall's name was always appearing as director of that outfit or this, never in a big way, but always there, owner of a hotel with a tax-evading accountant, major domo of a now thriving computer firm which stole software ideas. He was like a growing blob of mercury on the desk: if Ryan touched, he slid away, and if he hit, the droplet broke into a shower of smaller drops, easily reunited. But having sensed the rotten core, Ryan was not about to give up. A man could not be that bad without somehow breaking the law. Simply a question of finding how he had done it and how to prove it, and all he had got so far was the thumbs down from Simeon Churcher and a writ for the Commissioner. And the tortured memory of Annie's face transfixed with misery, the innocence which he himself had smirched finally turned into total disillusion. She might, just might, have got better without that. Might have written him off like any other girl, dusted herself down, got on with it. No chance now. Absently, Ryan bit his lip, and punched one calloused fist into his palm.

It would have been better if his conscience had been clearer in other, more professional respects, or if he had been warned less often of the dangers of keeping secrets, instead of pretending to investigate fraud while investigating something else. There had been this wife, see? Mrs Tysall, who used Harrods like a corner shop – well, she would, wouldn't she, nothing nearer. A brilliant looking redhead, weeping in the nick, stinking of frightened sweat and Chanel perfume, battered, bruised and bleeding. Twice, was it? Or more than twice, he couldn't remember. Statement taken, not usual from such quality, 'My husband tried to kill me,' touch. 'Why, madam?' 'I tried to go out ...' But as usual, be it the rich or the council house wife, allegation withdrawn within days. No proceedings, please. I daren't. Besides, we've made it up. Me complain? Never. Silly me. And then the Tysall wife had disappeared, simply disappeared off the face of the earth, or at least the pretty complexion of Knightsbridge. Nothing to investigate: no one reported her missing, no power to ask questions and interfere with the civil liberties of the husband.

'Seen the wife recently, have you?' Ryan had asked with his irritating wolfish grin, determined to needle that imperturbable face while pillaging Tysall's office under warrant for documents to show to Malcolm Cook. Charles smiled back, replied with bored dignity. 'She lives elsewhere, Mr Ryan. No business of yours. Have you finished?'

Ryan paused, smoked and slumped. He hadn't told Malcolm Cook about the Tysall wife saga, or about the other evidence of dismembered female lives, didn't trust him enough. Cook might have guessed, not entirely, and it was important he did not yet know that Ryan was not really pursuing a fraudsman thief, while Ryan knew he was chasing the tail of something worse. A psychopath possibly, a murderer almost certainly. Whatever Tysall was, it was dangerous. They didn't know the half of it.

Ryan piled and bound the reports, flicking back the last for a quick squint at Steepel's picture, taken from the flat, must be returned to relatives, but not if they failed to ask. Odd time for her to die. He'd spoken to her by phone the day before, thought again how strange it was with the educated ones, how it was they couldn't bring themselves to put down the phone on you even when they didn't want to speak. Too polite. His mind jumped over the photograph. Redhead, lovely curly redhead. Mrs Tysall, dead according to his instincts, redhead. With a great gulping need for life, gasping for the stuff, even as he had seen her, grasping at life, bruised but not beaten. Women like that don't disappear, not until they die.

Pity for them. Put out a general alert for all red-haired women of suitable age to steer clear of this bastard. Stay away, or number your days, he thought, while I think what the fuck to do next. Fraud, he supposed. A waste of time, he thought, with Tysall at large.

Charles Spencer Tysall was home early. No longer was he forced to work all hours, although the days when he had done so were still fresh in his mind as an exercise in stamina he never wanted to repeat. Speculation, clever investment in desperate companies forced to sell for less than their capital assets, sold at monumental profit or kept for more, all of that had ensured a measure of security, and he was nothing if not flexible in talents of management and acquisition. He liked to dabble, and the businesses he retained as director were varied enough for all his tastes. And they worked. Everything worked if you were creative about the means. There was his menage: Ted Plumb, the ex-detective, one or two tame lawyers, what more did he need? Somewhere in twenty years' achievement he had also laid hands on the Porsche, the Knightsbridge flat, the Paris house in the same sweep, and had mislaid one wife, or that was how he explained it.

Poor Porphyria. She was called Elisabeth, but he had always called her Porphyria, the only thing he had never really owned in forty-five years, never known or entirely subdued. Since Elisabeth's departure he had seen her in the streets, pursued her auburn image across counters and roads wherever sunlight had fallen on hair, and finally he had found her. Not her, perhaps, but certainly her graven image. She would live in this house with him, stay still without rebellion. This new Porphyria would learn from the old, would surely know better than risk Charles's style of combat. Wherever she was now, Madame Tysall the first must still bear the scars, and Charles shook with the memory of his own anger.

Unhappy reflections shuddered away. Charles changed from his immaculate suit into cords and rough silk shirt, then sat in his leather armchair with the cold bottle of Sancerre at his side. Knightsbridge rush-hour hummed softly below the second-floor windows of the mansion flat, sounds dimmed to pleasant indifference by the double-glazed windows. The room was lined with books and marbled paper. The carpet was rose red, Charles's choice, not that of the dear departed who enjoyed neither that colour nor the olive Chesterfield which complemented it. Not a visible hair of woman or dog, nor a single speck of dust on the floor. All trace of her was expunged. He had even told Ted to destroy the wretched puppy she had loved so much it had become her inseparable companion. Now there was simply the red carpet, at home with the black speakers which relayed the spindly Mozart sounds softly into his ears. Above the marble fireplace a gilded Georgian mirror showed Charles's dark-skinned face, green eyes below thick-arched brows as black as the raven-coloured hair, a mouth chiselled rather than sensual, the chin cleft. Truly a very beautiful man, with the broad shoulders and long legs of a dancing prince. Such a beautiful man, reminiscent of every dark hero in paperback romances. Slim-hipped, strong brown fingers, arresting face, full of hidden authority, with that luminous power of masculine saints depicted in sacred portraits, mesmeric eyes and the charm of the devil. Penetrating gaze, sensitive, perfect manners, superbly cast and presented for the diplomatic role of a Pontius Pilate.

Charles sipped the Sancerre, not waiting for Maria, simply expecting her. When the entry-phone buzzed from the street he did not rise, but pressed the electric device by his chair, and sipped another mouthful. She would sense the nature of his mood from the fact that the door was not locked and he did not rise to greet her. She could sense his exact requirements by the fact that she found him seated, would know how limited her time. Maria knew his habits and never commented, would not have considered argument. She had the advantage of a regular call-girl. Now he had tied her up with Ted Plumb, bodyguard, bruiser and private law-breaker, they were both his creatures, suitably afraid of him.

Into the room she slipped almost soundless, darker, smaller, slighter than he, a radiant Filipino, more smiles than words.

''Lo, Charlie boy. Happy today?'

'Not particularly. Pleased to see you. I needed you.'

'Oh good, Charlie boy.'

He stood then and took off her coat. Maria giggled and squirmed a little as he ran his hands over the smooth-sided dress, shuffled off her high-heeled shoes, raised her arms to the fastening behind her dress, revealing the absence of underclothing around her small breasts. Charles turned to his bedroom, undressed more slowly, watching her stretch like a dancer on the silk cover, her black hair around her. The image of a skinned rabbit briefly crossed his mind, swiftly dismissed as he lay beside her.

She moved to his side, ran her fingers across his flat belly, listening to his even breathing as she lay with her face against his chest. Then she bit gently, tickled his nipples with her fingers. He did not kiss her. Instead he fondled her neck, and pushed her head downwards. Without further prompting, she obeyed, one hand kneading the inside of one thigh while her mouth found her target, crouched above it, held in small fingers as she began a delicate circular motion with her tongue, slowly, then quicker, waiting for the imperceptible signs which would show his pleasure. Charles lay still, already removed to the evening ahead, admiring the cornice on the high ceiling, his thoughts absent from the work of her mouth apart from the automatic arching of his back and the moist sounds. As the sensation grew, he arched further, felt her pull back, pulled her head down savagely by the hair.

And held it there, silently, throughout his own climax, and her choking, panicking struggle.

There were times when Maria might have spat back, although she did not contemplate it now. What did it matter, beautiful clean boy. Better this fear, this coughing and mouthful of molten, waxy filth than all those sudden spurts of hate for the fat dirty uglies who actually tried to please. Sometimes, on a good day, Charlie boy was normal. Other days he would practise on her like a man tuning a violin, testing her body for sensation and himself for skill until she had arched three times and lay gasping like a fish filleted alive. Other times he wanted almost nothing, or made her crawl between his fine legs, like a harem-slave. So what? He always paid, always tipped and had never struck her – well, not hard. Not yet. She thought of Ted, Charles's regular henchman, and her inept lover, so undemanding by comparison. She thought of Ted, and smiled at their mutual master.

'On the hall table,' Charles said drowsily, hands crossed behind his head, lazily watching her dress.

'Thank you, Charlie boy. Next Thursday, yes?'

'I'll telephone if not.'

'OK, Charlie boy.' Consistent clients were hard to find. She scooped the notes from the inlaid table by the front door and left, high heels clicking down the stone corridor into a grateful silence. Once out of earshot, she ran. Maria never knew why she ran from Charlie boy's flat, but she always did.

In the silence, Charles showered, then returned to his

chair, the cool Sancerre, the music and the unfashionable volume of Browning. Poetry was his unwinding. Reading Browning he would think of nothing else. Not even the new lover would come to know all he had ever learned and enjoyed from the Marias of his world. There would be her image in his mirror, one day soon, owned, as he owned the mirrors in every room, where she would stand before him even now. In the meantime, he would make do with a passion for poetry, turn his eyes to verse for the appropriate images for a lighthearted mood. Browning, underrated in twentieth-century terms apart from his affair with that suitably dutiful daughter, Elizabeth Barrett. Effortless poet, renowned for romance, cynical to the core, or so it seemed for all that. Charles read the poetic plays for early-evening soothing, the stray poems with his aperitif, and turned to 'Porphyria's Lover', the oddest of them all, for light amusement.

> ... at last I knew
> Porphyria worshipp'd me; surprise
> Made my heart swell, and still it grew
> While I debated what to do.
> That moment she was mine, mine, fair,
> Perfectly pure and good: I found
> A thing to do, and all her hair
> In one long yellow string I wound
> Three times her little throat around,
> And strangled her. No pain felt she;
> I am quite sure she felt no pain.
> As a shut bud that holds a bee.

73

Good Porphyria, happy child who died so sweetly in the arms of a master, without pain. There was one imperfection in the mention of a golden head – he could not admire such flaxen hair – but even flawed, the poem always made him shake with quiet laughter, a familiar joke, but never stale. Soft, artistic hands against skin, his own curled around the neck of his wife, the disgusting vision of her bulging eyes and silent, resistant scream. One day, he was confident, the new and improved facsimile of the old would seat herself upon his lap, Porphyria-like, with graceful back towards him, her trust a feature of a perfect, faithful wife. Unlike the old, Miss Fortune would change her name. Her own, cheap title was not fit for an auburn swan. Soon she would see sense and stop avoiding him. Each has its fate, and he, of course, was hers.

Charles looked at his watch. Ted Plumb had begun his observation today; no doubt he would finish at six. Unless she began to co-operate soon, he would have to get Ted to look at her house. Ted was a faithful hound, and did as he was told.

Arriving home light-headed with exhaustion, Sarah found herself waiting for the dawn, the effect of tiredness so acute it made her wakeful, active, loathing the idea of sleep and all the exhaustion of waking into another day. Better stay awake at five in the morning, a perfect and precious peace, which reminded her she could cope with everything except fatigue. Even that was possible when grit-filled eyes watched the beginnings of light invading the windows, and the whole place clean and washed in that pale morning glow from the milky mist outside. Sarah shed her clothes, wandered naked as a baby in her own rooms. Alive. She wanted to postpone sleep for the hour of idle happiness and the regret which was bound to follow the lack of it. In these hours, uninhibited by clothes, she had been known to clean floors, polish silver, scour cupboards in a happy awareness of timelessness and order.

The wide crescent outside, full of early Victorian mansions, was an avenue of silent doors and swaying trees, her own for one silent hour. No hint of engine noise, one far-off trumbling train, yak yak, sleepily over the North London line, somnolent carrying of goods, too soon for human stock. Not even a motorcycle messenger or paperboy. Drawn to her large front windows, still naked, she watered the geraniums fading for water while she spoke encouragement. In the pinkening glow of five-thirty, she heard footsteps, ducked, and craned over the balcony, resting her chin on the cold iron curves of the rail, watching and curious. Down the park came the jogger, padding softly, breathing easily in sweat-stained black tracksuit, looking like a burglar returning home. Rhythmic pad-padding up the middle of the road without competition from machine or beast, a long, lithe body, moving with a smooth, slow sprint as effortless and elegant as a horse trotting back to the paddock having won the race without waiting for the cheers, owned by no one. His private time as well as hers: she ducked further below the ironwork in case he should see himself observed. There was a mild familiarity in those fine features which puzzled her in his quick upward glance. He had shimmied to a slow-breathing halt beneath her window, felt for the keys strung around his neck, passed

75

a large hand through thick, sweat-damp hair before jogging up the steps to the front door, impervious or indifferent to observation. Sarah could not recall where she had seen him before. New flat dweller, perhaps, using the side door to this largish block, while she always used the door in the centre. She was sometimes ashamed of how little she knew of her neighbours, pleased they knew so little of her. Jogger in black had the look of some woman's lover. May they go safely back to bed, where she, pursuing the freedom of restlessness, had been wakeful for half the night.

CHAPTER FIVE

'Don't know why you do this, Sarah, I really don't.'

Joan was truculent, grateful in an embarrassed, furious fashion which did not allow her to sound grateful at all. 'You don't bloody have to, you know.'

'I know I don't.' Sarah spoke with mild nonchalance as if she did not care either way. 'Can't have you dying for lack of sleep though, can I? Besides, I like him. Wouldn't have you for the day if I didn't, would I, Jack?'

'No,' said Jack, beaming at her.

'That's all right then,' said Joan, cuffing him lightly, speaking grumpily. 'Mind you behave. Bring him back if you're fed up. See you.'

The door had closed behind them with a hollow crash which echoed down the stone stairs, Joan both angry and relieved. So long as you don't think you're doing me any favours. Don't think I'm grateful, but God, I needed the peace. Why does she know when I'm at my wits' end, knows to arrive out of the blue and take one of them off me? How does she know? I don't bloody tell her. I could kill her for knowing, I really could, letting her do it . . . Little sod'll have a better day than he would cooped up with me, shame on me. Just don't let her think I can't cope . . .

The wind was blowing, stiff and hot. Sunday, Sarah's favourite day, improved by Jack, aged seven years and three precious months, relinquished into her care for a whole day through an offer of hers made with deliberate diffidence, accepted in the same vein. Free of the mother's watching eye, they were almost happy.

'Come on, Jacko! Race you!'

'Not yet. Sarah, what's Mummy doing?'

'She's at home, Jack. You know she is, you big softy.'

'Yes, but what will she be doing?'

'Sitting down, I think, with her feet up. Where we left her, probably asleep by now.'

'Will she be there when we get back?'

'When is she ever not? What's the matter, Jack?'

'If she goes to sleep she won't go in and tidy up my bedroom, will she? Then she can't find her birthday present, can she?'

'Is that all? Look at me, Jack.'

He paused, scuffed the new shoes she had bought him on the path, sighed and quivered. Jack suffered terribly for his sins, then he burst.

'Oh, Sarah, I ate the sweets you bought me last time to go with the present. Only some of them, then they were all gone.

She'll find the paper.' Tears were gathering in his big pale eyes. No wonder he wouldn't eat. Sarah bent to his seven-year-old level and put her arms round him. He was a prickly little boy, but he put his arms behind her neck and wept into her collar. Spindly boy, over-anxious, protective of his single parent, and as far as sweets were concerned, the same as any child who saw them rarely and wanted them all the time. Sarah was angry with herself. Her own kindness was both brusque and cunning towards this household, but it should not have been insensitive enough to cause any distress. She should have known better. The devastation of tears was rare in Jack's life; normally he was far too well controlled.

'Jack, listen to me, you dope. It's not so bad. Sweeties are meant to be eaten, and I shouldn't have left them with you. Mummy won't know and I bet she wouldn't mind if she did. Anyway, you've still got the talcum powder and stuff to give her. You haven't eaten them as well, have you?'

A watery smile emerged with some reluctance. 'That's silly.'

'Well then, we'll soon make it better.' She wiped his eyes, handed him the handkerchief to blow his nose. 'Tell you what we do. We go to the lake, then the other lake, and on the way back, we buy some more sweets. The ones she likes. We'll get them wrapped up, just the same as the others. Only lots of Sellotape.'

'I'm not supposed to take other people's money. Mummy told me.'

Sarah sighed. Mummy would. 'Look, when you're as big as me, you can pay it back.'

'Can I?'

'Sure can. I'll bop you on the head if you don't.'

'I will, I will, I will.' Drat the child, brought up with so much pride. She would like to make him naughty, rebellious and proud of himself.

She watched the thin legs kicking in front of her as she raced him up the hill to the Heath, relieved that the small distress was so easily cured. Not all Jack's problems had such easy remedies: there was little she could do about his father's defection, his mother's uphill struggle to survive. Joan was stiff-necked with pride, would take nothing smelling of charity, and ruled her offspring with a rod of iron. Unpaid bills and a rotten council estate were not going to turn them into delinquents, not as far as Joan was concerned. They would get an education if it killed her. Sarah knew them all, knew they deserved better, and did what surreptitious little she was allowed to do. The odd pair of shoes, the odd day out, anything she could sidle past the barrier of Joan's suspicion. She had endless patience; small children enchanted her. Charity did not, and unbeknown to Joan, she knew all about it.

They had climbed Parliament Hill to see the kites, run and rolled down towards the lakes, both of them breathless. This was a regular pilgrimage to see the fancy boats, chugging round the edges of the shallow pond, controlled by their owners from the shore. Serious recreation, power boats, remotely controlled, charged by Hampstead fathers and healthy-looking children. Looking like tramps by comparison, and without a boat of their own, both stood and watched, Jack with his usual innocent curiosity, untinged by envy, full of wonder.

'Look at that one,' he whispered.

Sarah looked, and saw a man and a boy, tall, well-dressed father ordering a sturdy blond son to behave. Yards from the edge, their battery boat was idling and they could not get it back. Like a pretty, disobedient animal, it floated in splendour, refusing all instructions. Papa's irritation was all too clear. The child was sulky. The boat inched further away. Jack looked at Sarah and Sarah looked at Jack, and they both began to giggle. There was nothing funnier than impotent fury.

Then, as the man turned to gesture, Sarah recognised the face of Belinda Smythe's husband, one-time host of more than two years since, a souvenir of lately married days and married friends. The recognition was mutual: both paused until Martin Smythe's face cleared, lost its irritation and took on the glow of remembered manners. The widow Fortune, always fancied her. Didn't remember them having a son. Confusion needing enlightenment, must tell Belinda.

'Sarah, isn't it? Not seen you for ages. This one yours?'

'Hallo, Martin. No, not mine. Wish he was.' There never had been much to say.

'Trouble with the boat then? This is Jack . . . '

'And this is Benjamin. He's cocked it up.'

The two seven-year-olds looked at one another with mutual suspicion. Jack grinned: if in doubt he always grinned. Benjamin grinned with less certainty: he was more at home with adults.

'I didn't cock it up,' he protested to Sarah. 'We need Uncle Malcolm.'

'If you say that one more time, Ben, I'll scream,' his father warned through gritted teeth. 'He means Malcolm Cook,' he added to Sarah in explanation. 'Remember Malckie? You both came to dinner once, I seem to remember. Fat Malckie. He always used to relieve us of our children on Sunday afternoons. Perhaps we took him too much for granted, but he seems to have disappeared. Bloody nuisance really. Malckie was a natural with kids.'

Benjamin was restless, growing truculent. 'The boat. Daddy, it's going further ... ' Sarah felt Jack's hand creep into her own, gently pulling her on. They were all suddenly uncomfortable. Martin gazed distractedly at the expensive toy, moving further and further out of reach.

'You must come and see us again, Sarah. Soon.'

They moved away, turned to wave, and saw father and son devoted to argument, the chortle of laughter from Jack hiding Sarah's lightning blush. Of course she remembered Malcolm Cook, never quite forgot him. Malcolm with the big gentle hands, his clear, understanding mind, his instinctive way with children. She would not think of Malcolm Cook, mere memory of other days, one last sharing begun with a kind of compassionate experiment of her own, ending in the last real conversation before she had slipped away wilfully into her own self-sufficient world, unfit to help him then. She had run before he could touch her or make her vulnerable, determined he should not. She could not afford it. She had not wanted to know ever again what that was like. Or even what it was like to be with a man who seemed to understand so much, despite the earlier clowning. Another outsider,

82

surprised by nothing. Don't think of it now. Both of them licking wounds, and he too gone into hiding from the conventional world. A couple of freaks, giving freakish comfort.

'I'm glad,' said Jack, relinquishing her hand to brandish his own in the air, 'that I haven't got things like that boat. Costing plenty, and then getting lost. I'd be very worried, all the time. Do you know what I mean?'

'Yes I do, pet. Very well. Is it time to find a sweet shop?'

He grinned again and began to run, whooping and jumping. She followed faster, the red hair streaming out behind her, shouting with him, circling round him, letting him win.

Far behind, a large shambly figure stubbed out his cigarette, coughed, swore and followed. Ted Plumb could not understand it. In the distant but far from dim days of Drugs Squad observations, Ted had learned to control surprise. There he would be, stamping his feet on a cold afternoon, wondering if he could slope off for a drink and cover it carefully in his notes, when suddenly the least likely suspect, supposed to be miles away, would pop out of a back door like a genie, and force him to move. Surprise would have been confined to a curse on the breath, his body immobile against shock, as it was now.

He had left the bloody dog at home, and now he was grateful. Jack might have recognised it, just as Ted so clearly recognised Jack, his own son, romping over the grass with the pretty woman he had been ordered to follow. Well, well. The same woman who had such a preference for adult company, dressed for her men, smiled at them, playing here with a penniless boy. She certainly was versatile. He shrugged.

No point being curious about it. He'd find the connection in time, but the sight of his own child was hardly a comfort, even to a man as bereft of paternal instinct. He had better not mention any personal interest in his report to Charles Tysall; besides, he was sure he was not supposed to report activities of such studied innocence as these. What the girl did with males of Jack's age was of no interest to Charles. Perhaps this woman lived near his own wife, perhaps that explained it, but he felt acute annoyance. He had supposed she was simply another of Tysall's targets, but what the hell was she doing with a child not her own, making Ted so impatient an observer, and even making him begin to like her?

He watched the boy, sighed and turned away. Let them be, but he wanted them back, some of the time. Not all of the time; not when he was in bed with Maria, but when he was out in the streets with that damn dog, going home to the bare room in Hackney, then he did. At least he had Maria. This woman, richer, peculiarly beset by gentlemen friends, had no one to call her own. Go home now. Nearly closing time. With surprising speed and neat steps, soft-shoed Ted ducked away, turned his feet towards the houses and the first drink of the day.

Sarah watched the flying figure of skinny Jack. Look at him compared with the elegance of little Benjamin Smythe. Fatherless, not quite rudderless Jack, just like me. Well, you little monster, don't grow up obeying all the rules, will you? Not worth it. Be yourself. Whatever else you do. Hope someone, maybe me if I get the chance, makes sure you shout when it hurts rather than lie down and cry so easy. See

84

yourself in a mirror and punch the rest in the eye if they don't like it. She shrugged, and ran after him. 'Wait for me, Jack . . . Wait for me . . . ' Sunday children, better by far than none.

When Malcolm Cook had next been invited to dine with Belinda and Martin three weeks after the time he had with Sarah Fortune, he had demurred. He had almost been rude, and deliberately obtuse.

'Have you invited that girl, you know who I mean, Sarah?'

'Sarah who? Oh, widow Sarah. No. Should we?'

'You invite whoever you like. Only, she gave me a lift home.'

'Nice girl, Sarah, but we do try to vary the list. Apart from you, of course. She's very quiet, Sarah.'

Malcolm paused. Not as he remembered, with his whole size quivering slightly at the memory. He must not ask after her, he must not pursue her. She had been quite clear.

'Well, my dears.' The old heartiness took over. 'Afraid I can't oblige your kindness. On a diet. Besides, very busy. May be absent for a while.'

'For how long, Malckie?' She sounded annoyed. 'The children will be impossible.'

'I'm sorry,' he said formally. It sounded as if he was going away for a long time. Visions of Captain Oates, as he walked out of Scott of the Antarctic's tent, floated into his mind. 'I may be gone for some time . . . ' With his present stones of weight, and smaller stores of bravery, Malcolm felt he would have lasted longer than Oates. Easier to be brave when you knew you had no choice. Oates had meant them to use his supplies. Malcolm wished his surplus fat could be distributed with so much fairness, and felt the old familiar longing for company, any kind.

He felt he might give at the seams of himself with the sheer grief of his own rage, and in this deficient life of his, something would have to go. The bloody bulk of it. He smiled the first smile of the day at his own pun. Inside the reflection of his own size, normality had beckoned like a mirage not dignified yet by any real belief in it.

Two years forward and tidying his new flat, a different man moved easily from room to room, drastically altered despite the fact that he still expected the sight of his own flesh to crowd his mirror. It was strange to recall how much he had hated his new determination when he first began. How he had crawled up the steps to the front door of the old place at the end of that first, short run with his stomach trembling, his thighs quivering, calves on fire, a throbbing in his head and a hazy dizziness blinding his eyes along with the sweat which ran down from his hair. The two flights which led to the old flat seemed the last, impossible obstacle, and he had imagined the whole world must be aware of the deafening sound of his own breathing. All that for a stumbling run of two hundred yards, and the sight of the neighbour behind the first-floor net curtain, giggling at the sight of his comical distress, wondering between times whether she ought to call an ambulance. Poor fat sod, what did he think he was trying to do? Being fat was like being old, he had discovered whilst soaking in the bath, a dying whale, and waiting for the sickness to pass. All attempts to change it are regarded as inherently stupid and undignified. They were both of those, but no more than the condition.

'You must be mad, Mr Cook,' said the doctor, faced across the surgery table next evening as Malcolm eased himself off the chair like an invalid, paralysed by stiffness. 'Man of your age and weight suddenly trying to sprint. You'll give yourself a heart attack. Try diet first. A little gentle movement, perhaps.'

'I'm not a geriatric,' Malcolm had said mildly. 'No,' snapped the small thin medical man. 'Nor a child. Most people begin by touching their toes.'

But he could not start so slowly. Malcolm could not do the thing in stages. He would have to charge at it painfully, stocky bull at five-bar gate, ignoring slow and sensible progress. Whatever he did must hurt, show results, require courage. Gradual progression would be like watching the clock for the second-hand of failure. Malcolm ran again, then again, forcing himself further by one more street, hating the process as he had never hated anything, loathing the disabling stiffness which followed. He ran in the dark, spending the hours of light inventing excuses for not persisting, until he moved himself to the mirror to taunt his own fat cowardice, and, suitably disgusted, fled the house in running-shoes, into rain, sleet, warmth or thunder, not noticing or caring which.

Cruel laughter in the office. 'Have you heard? Cook's dieting . . . Lost an ounce so far.' He heard, and tried to smile.

The second reaction, after the sheer horror at the pain of it, was a wonder in the discovery of the ability to move on the day when he woke without groaning, suddenly able to put one foot on the ground out of his bed without the rest following in a slow and clumsy roll. Wonder, mixed with curiosity about the next stage. Could he move better, stand taller, stride out with more economy? How fast would he be able to go, and how far? In retrospect, he realised it was this burning curiosity which made him persist far more than the simple desire to be thin. Then there was another stage, one of intoxication after he had shuffled, run, jogged one whole mile. The stage when he knew with absolute conviction he would crack it even if it took forever, and one day he would be free of all this bulk. That marked the beginning of an obsession, a voyage of exploration across boundaries of pain, stiffness and teasing, through mindless mornings, hungry afternoons and breathless evenings, to see how far he could take himself and what lay on the other side. No time for dinner party clowning. But when Malcolm Cook emerged after several months looking an approximation of a normal plump human being there was no time for him either. He found the lightness of his frame had allowed him to move from half-way up the pinnacle of loneliness, occupied in bearable isolation, to a point at the summit where the air was very thin indeed, and no one pretended to know him at all.

Belinda and Martin were the first casualties. He knew too much, had been told too much, fat father confessor, and who could now confide in a thinner man, or weep on his shoulder? 'It isn't the same bloke,' said Belinda. 'Not the same at all.' Such an ordinary man could not tell jokes with the same wonderful pomposity as a fat man. Their parties could not cope with a clown *passé*. Other friends thought long and hard. They decided to avoid him, and finally decreed: Falstaff, be thou not thin. Your role was made for a fat man, you are a disappointment to us all. He was the same generous man, but they did not like him. He made them uncomfortable, and he found he did not like them much either, although there was nothing else to replace them. So Malcolm simply retreated into himself. Not comfortable, but not despised. Shrouded in work, saturated with all the antisocial knowledge of the criminal world, he lived alone.

The dramatic weight-loss, and the emergence of a startlingly good looking son, worried Mrs Penelope Matthewson, who was having a difficult day, made infinitely worse by the fact that her only son, product of a brief and difficult marriage, had been missing for months and had installed an answerphone. She had not known what to say when faced with its pleasant message, spoken clearly in his familiar friendly voice, and she had only suppressed the instinct to chatter after the whining noise when she had realised that the message was the sum-total of the response, leaving her shouting into a vacuum and feeling silly, still full of irritated affection.

Penelope wanted forgiveness from her son for her neglect of his childhood, and knew she had it. She was grateful for Ernest's great love for his stepson, and irritated by that too. Swallowing pride, she dialled again, listened this time, and left a message after the bleep. 'Malcolm, I know you're there.' (Although she had no idea why she knew.) 'Phone me when you can. I need to see you. I'm very worried about Dad.'

He did not telephone. He arrived instead, adding to the guilt and still shocking her with his new appearance, even as her own, equally unerring instinct guided her not to comment, forced her to smile as if she did not find him changed. Malcolm, fat from the overfed age of eight, shovelled from pillar to post among the debris of a marriage, and away to school at the age of eleven where he grew fatter and learned to survive on his wits, was the thinnest she could ever remember, slender, fit and athletic.

'Dear God,' she said, swaying in the doorway, smile frozen, 'you're even thinner. Would you like to eat now or later?' When he did not smile, she began to laugh at his handsome face, so like the mulish small-boy look he had worn when pushed too far, relieved to find him so familiar. 'Oh, Malcolm darling. You look wonderful. You make me understand why I fell in love with your father. Come in.'

He grinned at last. 'One condition.'

'What's that?'

'No food. You got me into this, don't hinder me getting out.'

She hugged him, melted her sweet-smelling arms around his neck, and led him in. Plump feet in plump shoes dinting the velvet carpet. Mrs Matthewson had never liked modern things or sharp angles, nothing harsh to the touch, even in the days when she had been Mrs Cook with a husband as liberal and progressive as her own Ernest was not. She sat opposite her son on a sofa which almost enveloped her in high colours of hummingbirds. The curtains matched, the walls reflected the soothing and vibrant colours, like the woman herself.

Penelope never admitted Malcolm was a mistake, but in a life now devoted to comfort and order, she wished she had produced a child of more predictable qualities, or one her second husband loved less. But in those dimmer days, Pen had always reserved the greatest devotion of life for the two husbands. Now she loved this son and this husband equally, and wished they would damn well do the same. She looked quizzically at Malcolm. Something was all wrong with the boy, and she knew by that smile of his, a wonderful smile, enlivened by enormous affection, curtailed by equally huge reserve, that she had better not ask what it was, for fear of an answer. In turn, he had sunk into a large, exquisitely comfortable chair, and was thinking with only the slightest regret how odd and spartan his own life had become in comparison to this, and to all his dear mama would want for him.

'How's Father?' Noticing her fidgeting with the desire to present him with the large measure of Scotch which greeted all visitors, and which she knew he would refuse.

'Not well. I'm worried. Will you come and talk to him?'

'Mother, you know I can't. He won't take advice from me. Not since I've refused to take it from him, insulted him by refusing to join the practice. He's never forgiven me, dabbling in crime, humble prosecutor paid by the state, and he won't confide in me now.'

'But, Malcolm ... you could try at least ... '

'Yes, I could. But only if he asks. Not otherwise. Come on, Ma, you know him. If he came in now, crippled with an ulcer, he'd start the same old argument within minutes. He can't help it. He'd ask how I was, slap me on the back, and say, "When are you coming into the firm, then?" Again. And I'd say, "You know me, Dad. I'm a loner, always was. Can't work for anyone. Better off with crooks and coppers, drunks and thieves," and so we'd go on until he sank into silence and me into mindless jokes. If I could get him to talk naturally, we might have a chance of being able to talk about himself, but then again, only if he would. And could.'

'He loves you, Malcolm. You know he does. I don't know why, you aren't even his, but he does.'

'You make it sound like an accusation.'

'Well, no. Yes. I mean . . . No, I don't mean anything. I mean I simply wish pleasing him wasn't so difficult for you. I try to understand; part of me does, part of me doesn't. I just want you both happy.'

Heavy tears gathered and slid solidly down her round pink cheeks before she brushed them away in frustration. Penelope was not a regular weeper. She would stoop to black-mail of most sorts, but not weeping.

'Mother, don't. It isn't me making him unhappy. It's the firm that makes him miserable. He made it, but he doesn't belong anymore in a big commercial partnership full of whizz-kid lawyers when he really belongs in the library, dispensing common sense over half-moon specs, giving out inspired pats on hand and "don't be so silly" kind of advice which never needs a law book. He always said he couldn't be bothered with law books because they were all print and no pictures, a bit like me really, but his kind of lawyer isn't in fashion. He's all at sea with the technical age. They haven't even got time for lunch. He might think he'd feel more comfortable with me in the room next door, but he wouldn't. Get him out more, encourage all his other interests.'

A smile broke through Pen's creased concern, and she was cheered by the prospect of positive action. 'Get married, Malcolm,' she said, unable to leave him with the last word. 'Provide us with a couple of grandchildren. We're both broody.'

He rose, dropped a kiss on her brow. 'Chance would be a fine thing,' he answered lightly.

Penelope continued, speaking to herself as much as to him. 'There's a gorgeous girl in the office, one of the young ones. Ernest has a crush on her. I pretend it annoys me for the sake of form, but I know it's not that kind of crush. She's a daughter-substitute. She stops him feeling lonely by being the only one there who can begin to think like him, or understand it. Besides, she helps me look after him. She keeps me informed,' she added darkly.

'Spies in the camp?' queried Malcolm. 'Not sure I like the sound of that.'

'No, no, no . . . she's no sneak. Not the school-prefect type at all. She simply understands him. When he gets upset, you know the way he does, she calms him down, and when the ulcer is on the march, she tells him jokes and stops him going on the rampage. Whenever his secretary threatens to resign, the others call her in and she makes them see the storm will pass, and makes them laugh. They talk about anything and everything, and when he's really on the warpath to the tune of risking another heart attack, she phones me up and warns me.'

'No secrets?'

'If he tells her any, she would never tell me, and if Ernest tells her anything about the firm, she wouldn't tell anyone else. She only tells me when he's really over-excited. I trust her. Lovely voice. Penelope, she says to me, this is an early gale-warning, and I'll know to give him a big hug when he gets back, to show he's still king in his own house. And a good supper. And not argue.'

'He's a lucky man. Surrounded by adoring women.'

'But not adoring stepsons.'

Silence fell into the sunlight passing through the curtains across Penelope's fresh flowers and her bonny, anxious face. Malcolm wished he could please her more, please them both, herself and the irascible stepfather he loved so much. Wished he had the means to restore that volatile old man to contentment. 'He has good friends,' Malcolm said firmly, watching the sunbeams dance on the polished wood. Pen looked at them too, pleased by the effect, secretly gratified to see her son discomfited. 'I must clean the windows,' she remarked, one of her *non sequiturs* which closed the conversation on family topics. It was always closed before she admitted too much. Malcolm was resigned to it. He knew she could not say there was more than that in Ernest's current high anxiety. Some client, some breach of his old-fashioned honour, some arrow lodged in his keen conscience, festering, which Malcolm could have discovered and she could not.

She sighed and rose slowly. She could not say more today, and this was not, as she had hoped, the best time to suggest

94

to her only son the delightful prospect of a dinner at home, graced by a mellow stepfather and the lovely but suitable young woman. What this family needed was a decent daughter-in-law, a bit of romance, and Malcolm was thirty-three. He needed a wife.

Painting by numbers on the life of M. Cook was adroitly, respectfully resisted. He had fended off the far more serious questions concerning work and career by waxing lyrical to Mother on the subject of the new flat, although she sniffed at the very idea of living in one storey so far from the ground, couldn't fathom the appeal at all. 'Why not a house, Malckie, at your age?' She could not tell him all her fears any more than this son of hers could explain how he had emerged from the chrysalis of sixteen stone a strange, shy shadow of himself with no known place in the world, but full of silent fury, and acquiring some very eccentric habits indeed.

They always left their conversations incomplete, at the point where they should have started. It had become a habit.

'See you soon, darling.'

'Give my love to Father.'

'Of course.'

She moved to the kitchen for the therapy of cooking. Malcolm hurried to court for the therapy of crime. He would feel more at home there in the mess of files and accusations. And after court he would go on looking through the directories, make ten more phone calls. Malcolm was looking for Sarah Fortune. The process was slow, but absorbing enough to dismiss all thoughts of his family from his mind. This much he knew: she was a solicitor and a widow, but the Law Society could not help. No trace of Fortune, they said. She may practise, they explained, under her married name, but the registration will be under her maiden name, you see. If you don't know the maiden name, and she calls herself something else now, we cannot help. So, each day, time allowing, he rang another of the hundreds of legal firms in the Solicitor's Diary, to make his discreet inquiries. The response was often puzzled, the task embarrassing but necessary. Sighing, half in hope, half in frustration, he reached for the phone.

A long day, so filled with different preoccupations. Criminals, families, and the quest to find Sarah which had so far taken months, from the two years since he had seen her. And after this, his nightlife began, running the streets in darkness, looking for the man and the dog, regarding all he might see with his mild, forgiving eyes.

CHAPTER SIX

'You look like the nicest kind of sleepy cat. And I wish you didn't have to go.'

She smiled a wide smile, pulled a face in the middle of a graceful yawn.

'So do I, but there's just this little question of work in the morning.'

'It's only eleven. I'll get you a taxi. Stay on a minute. Talk to me.' He pulled her hand. She sat down next to him on the bed, half-dressed, nicely rumpled, obliging. Simeon's moves were all ponderous, not as heavy-handed as before, but she could still see him thinking ahead, like a child.

'Sarah?'

'Yes?'

'You know we agreed I wouldn't pry into your life. I've known you for three months now, and I feel a new man ...' He smiled at her fondly. 'I can hold a knife and fork, I don't

stop people smoking by waving things in their faces ...'
She stroked his head, and he grinned sheepishly. 'And I've
honoured the agreement, haven't I?' She nodded. 'Well, I
thought it gave me licence to ask. You don't have to answer.
But why, why be so secretive with your life? Even though you
seem content. You don't have to answer, but what made you?'

'Made me? Nothing made me.'

'I know that ... But why, then? Why be ...'

'Your mistress?' She dimpled.

'Your description. I rather like it. Every man should have a
mistress at one point in his life, perhaps. It honours me, your
description, but you aren't mine. And you are a lady, never
anything less.' Even in his dressing-gown, with his eyebrows
and hair pointing on end, like an endearing goblin, Simeon
had relearned the gallantry of his youth, and he meant it.

'Why do you want to know?' She was buttoning the sleeves
of a white blouse, the one she had worn into his house after
her official life, and now he watched as she reassumed that
other shape in front of his eyes, hiding herself in the good
black skirt, silk scarf and all the everyday uniform.

'I want to know because I like you,' he said simply. 'And
whatever our arrangement, I'd like to be counted as a friend.
Difficult thing to be if one's as ignorant as this. I know
some of the motivations, of course, but not all of them.
Tell me why.'

She sat again. One flick of the hairbrush through that red
mane and it would be too late, she would have become the
Sarah known to the Law Society, not the luminous-eyed
creature who, among other things, sang him songs and

insisted he learn how to cook. (When you're indoors, eat properly. Enjoy it.) And redecorate his flat: make yourself comfortable and you'll make others comfortable. No, don't undo what your wife did, just adapt it to your own taste. A motto to alter his life. Sarah's service was comprehensive. He often forgot the bedtime bit when faced with her subtle capacity for mending lives, often regretted the restrictive nature of the association, but he never once counted the expense which followed in the wake of it. His flat and himself glowed with new health and his face was alive with questions.

'All right. I'll tell you why. Briefly. An exercise in making a long story short.'

'Not too short.'

'Very short. Call it the reaction of a disillusioned widow with a career which bores her to death, a kind of prison. In order not to see the bars, needs uncomplicated relationships on equal terms, with everyone knowing where they are. Will that do?'

'Far from satisfactory.'

'It isn't really very much more complicated than that. I like doing what I'm good at. I like you. You're good company.'

'Sarah . . . What do you do on all the other evenings in the week when you don't see me?'

'Ah. Clean the windows, wash my socks, see friends and twiddle my thumbs. In other words, with all respect to your curiosity, nothing harmful and none of your business.' It was said inoffensively with the smile he could not resist.

'Tell me about your family.'

'Genteel, poorish, brutally religious. Wanted the best

for me. Threw me out with the onset of the first boyfriend. Forgave me for qualifying and marrying, a brief period of acceptance, but not for being widowed. Indecent, you see, bound to be my fault and very embarrassing for them. They always preferred my sister. Better I stayed away.'

In the calm tones, and although he lacked sensitivity, Simeon could sense undertones of terrible rejections, fights, abandonment. He hesitated.

'And your husband? What was he like? Did you love him?'

'Oh yes, I loved him, but he is a different story for another time. Not today.'

Nothing more detailed would follow. Simeon believed that widowhood was about as dignified as a poke in the eye, but did not see why it led to Sarah's solution of such a floating life. On the other hand, he could not see why not.

'You could always marry me, and give up the single status.'

'Don't be silly, Simeon my love. You know we'd never work on a daily basis, and anyway, you'll need a respectable wife. Someone really wifely, you know, someone intelligently normal. If you go for an appointment on the Bench, as well you might, you'll need a spouse beyond reproach, fit for all those Benchers' dinners and the occasional scrutiny of the press. Not a reprobate like me. Someone who would think like you and support everything you did.'

He sighed, thought of the outrage of the top table in the Inner Temple Hall, shook his head sadly. Too glamorous she was, and far too funny for that august company.

'There's nothing I dislike about you, Sarah, except your dreadful realism.'

'Kiss me goodbye, then.'

'Until next time,' he added quickly. 'I still need you. Don't forget the Ball. You haven't forgotten Gray's Inn Ball? Big occasion for me, the final test of my greatly improved manners. You said you'd think about it. You will come, won't you? Please?'

'Oh, I don't know, Simeon. I can't, really.'

He was openly distressed. 'Please, Sarah. I've been out of circulation for so long I won't manage without you. Just once. Please. Why not? Is the thought of an evening with me in public so terrible?'

Pretty terrible, thought Sarah, but only because of potential embarrassments which have nothing to do with your company.

'Why not?' he repeated, taking advantage of her sudden and surprising nervousness.

'Well, half my legal acquaintance and some of my clients go to this thrash. I shall feel exposed,' she added lamely.

'Exposed to what?'

He regarded her with innocence, his concern touching her as he took her hand. 'Exposed to what?' he said again. 'I'm sure you haven't done anything wrong.'

'No,' said Sarah. 'No, of course not. I haven't done anything wrong at all.'

'Well then, you'll come with me,' he said triumphantly. 'I'll look after you.'

No one, thought Sarah, has ever done that. And I shall go with him. He's a kind man, so unused to having an ally – I must help him swim in those crowds. There was a glimmer of resignation as well as mischief which Simeon found puzzling, but dismissed in his pleasure at her acceptance.

'I knew I would win in the end,' he said triumphantly. 'You'll enjoy it, and of course, it won't cost you anything.'

'It might,' she replied.

On her way home, Sarah forgot the prospect of the Ball, remembered Simeon's questions and regretted the luxury of words. What little she had said had been entirely true, but however bland, any form of confession weakened the self-sufficiency she carried before her like a talisman, and all the explanations had been contrived. She did not know why she was as she was or how she had so simply arrived at living as she did, alone but accompanied by the balm of constant activity. There were precious few clues in either past or present. Perhaps she was just a little wild. In any event, she hated introspection which nailed her down on the crucifix of the past for nothing. A good girl, such a good girl in childhood and marriage. Studious, anxious and abused for her earthy beauty in the early stages, utterly devoted in the second, pinioned by the constant desire to please. Sarah thought of her blond and muscular husband, the friends of his whose sophistication had puzzled and defeated her once. Maybe she had not been much fun then. Well, I am now, she thought. Now there is no one to disapprove, no one to look. As for Simeon, again, why not? Don't ask, do. There was nothing to it apart from all her lack of inhibition in contrast to all those dry and dreadful rooms of the law, where loneliness and frustration existed behind frozen smiles on faces refined by conventional success, masking personal agonies.

She would have no such agonies, would prefer to kiss and stroke such faces rather than accept their severity, preferred to touch rather than stand outside gracious windows looking in. No, there was no explanation to placate the logical mind of Simeon or anyone else who could not understand the simpler pursuits of pure pleasure, the freedom of choice granted by money, both seen as an end in themselves, a freedom. She was becoming eccentric, knew it and did not care. Without showing the symptoms of freakishness, she had always been the outsider who was never accepted. Nothing had altered except for the fact that she had given up trying. If in doubt, which was rare, Sarah followed base instinct, and felt the better for it without realising how. It was the sheer, determined joy in her which made her so attractive.

Sarah's taxi juddered to a halt outside her door, while the driver delivered the last of his homily on the troubles of married life. She had heard him sympathetically, listening from the outside in, standing on the edge, the way she always had, wondering why there was anyone left who kept to the rules. Envying them very little, there being no shred of envy in her, paying a large tip for the pleasure of being home.

Turning the corner of the street, jogging away from the basement entrance, Malcolm heard the taxi, turned back, padded on. Neighbours were neighbours. In the weeks of living above and alongside these, in his new flat, he had done his best to ignore their existence and they had reciprocated the indifference. As he skimmed over a patch of dirt, avoided the arms of a last drunken straggler from the pub on the corner, he did not care if his neighbours noticed him any more than he cared about the fact that he had become extremely odd, and if they were odd too, always coming home at midnight or three in the morning, so much the better.

The habit of running by night, generally only ever functioning by night at all, coasting by day on a few hours' sleep, working on auto-pilot, had become entrenched. He was sure now it was his chosen work, as much as his bulk, which had pushed him to the edge of the world. Sympathetic criminal lawyers, like policemen, know too much, and he knew himself to be uncomfortable company in the civilised world. Very little human society intruded on his isolation, and those who did were filtered by the answerphone. When all those slept, along with his neighbours, Malcolm came to life. Like Dracula, he thought. Once fat Dracula.

In the terms of his own description, defined by the friendly policeman who stopped him twice and with whom he was now on waving terms, Sir had become addicted to neon-lighting, finding sunlight pale by comparison. The constable did not say it like that; he had merely remarked on how Malcolm obviously preferred the night-shift as he did himself, and warned him against muggers similarly fleet of foot. Malcolm agreed. He loved the scenery of the night, that great divide of city darkness between two disparate ways of life, two whole societies. Sometimes he would run twelve miles, around Hackney Marshes and the Lea Reservoir, then back, or up to Hampstead Heath, avoiding nocturnal lovers, but mostly he preferred the streets. He had been running now for almost two years, and he was as lithe and as self-possessed as a cat.

So far, this preference was no more eccentric than that of a policeman or night-security guard. But the darkness inspired Malcolm with mischief; he could understand, if not copy, the vandal's secret glee of midnight desecration, Kilroy with spray. I was here, I tell you, but now I'm not. Since he was not yet free of a law-abiding nature, although his sympathies had come to lie with those who had the opposite, most of the mischief was faintly philanthropic. The Rolls-Royce in the square, the one parked nightly by an arrogant owner to the maximum inconvenience of everything around it: letting down those expensive tyres three nights in succession before the guinea dropped, might have been juvenile, but hardly wicked. Sprinting down the back alley of the same rich square to find a burglar half-way into a window, warning him of the imminence of discovery without doing more, was an act of debatable charity, but Malcolm could only empathise with the wild-eyed creatures of the night.

For years, he had met them all by day; he knew them better than they knew themselves and had somehow lost the knack of condemning. Malcolm's job was to prosecute the lawbreakers, read of them, question them, only nobody had ever told him there might come a time when he would cease to see them as outsiders, feel more at home with them, even if he did not emulate them. Some of them, the regular car thieves, prowlers, dustbin-bag watchers, scavengers, saw him as a kind of harmless vigilante. Others, including the stray constable, knew different, and wondered how far he would regress. Those on the outside come to see nothing other than the outside.

Malcolm, reborn, became one of those completely at home in the midnight desert, blinking at dawn and the intrusion of light, and might well have forgotten even his sense of pity as his actions became more careless and his intervention more direct, if it had not been for the one regular sighting which niggled his bizarre contentment. Unlike the misplaced statues, the silly, changed direction signs, the other frivolous, absent-minded jokes he had played, there was no chance of humour with this pair. The man and his dog were a sight he had grown to dread in the last few weeks: both filled him with grief, the anger focusing on the man, leaving nothing but pity for the dog.

Always in the early hours, as if their respective needs could only be met long after midnight and without witnesses. A bulky man and scrawny animal, walking the mean Hackney streets, the only sight which, in Malcolm's growing indifference to humankind, almost provoked tears. A stocky man of indeterminate age, good clothes, but scruffy and careless, peculiarly light-footed, always more than slightly drunk or drugged, difficult to tell without smelling, as if this state, along with the hour, were a prerequisite to taking the dog for an impatient exercise which was far from a labour of love. On these swaying perambulations, the man muttered, grumbled and pulled with the dog's lead clenched inside his pocket, so that the animal danced, front paws scrabbling, strangled neck extended through every tortured step, whimpering for relief. 'Turn on him, bite him, and run away with me.' These were the instructions Malcolm formed in his mind, but he had never gone far enough to act. He saw them most nights, though not every night, and dreaded it, swaying, yelping, cursing in mutual suffering, man hating dog, but bound to each other. Burglars, sad prostitutes on Seven Sisters Road, some of whom waved and jeered at his useless custom whenever he passed, watching him waving and grinning back, all of them, theoretically at least, made some sort of choice. But poor bloody dog, he thought, did not enter the world with an owner's grudge, did not deserve it. Or a neck redraw from the pulling, or the lead. Or slow abuse and slower starvation, poor bitch.

You must not interfere unduly in the lives of others, even to save them, and thou shalt not steal. Authorities exist to prevent man's inhumanity to man or beast. Wasn't that the rule behind all his prosecutions, the criminal law bible, as well as the commandments of his own English schooling? Malcolm stood in front of his mirror, not a deliberate move, but the mirror was there in his bedroom. In it stood a vision of mangled dog, by the side of a slender, cowardly man. Himself. Mirrors always carried into his life accusations, premonitions and waves of disgust. Malcolm picked up a chair and hit the glass, watching it smash into smithereens, shattered picture of a hypocrite who could act daily to imprison lawbreakers, but could not even rescue a suffering dog. Tomorrow, then, he would deal with theft. The day after, or whenever he saw them next, he would commit it. After that, God knew what he might become. He did not particularly care, but old morals, old images, died hard. He was happier without the mirror.

CHAPTER SEVEN

'Just like old times, sir.' Ryan knew he sounded over-jovial.

Chief Superintendent Bailey grunted and eyed the walls. After the conference with counsel on the infinitely tedious subject of mortgage fraud, they had been aiming for the usual pub in Fleet Street opposite the High Court, the same gloomy place to which Ryan, Bailey and others had resorted with speed and several years of practice. Like camels, with the hump and the thirst, Ryan had said. Bailey, ex-Flying Squad, murder squads, and half the worst divisions in the Met, now basked in the relative predictability of Fraud, tinged with the quiet excitement of a late love affair, and these days rarely stayed out drinking. Not that Ryan imagined there was much temptation in a place like this. Bailey had shunned the regular haunt for its overpowering crowds, and they sat instead in the relative calm of the wine bar. Within minutes, the calm had been shattered by baby barristers baying for dry white wine. Ryan looked at his ice-cold continental lager. Not bad, for an arm and a leg. Man'd spend a fortune getting pissed in here, and he'd needed something stronger to duck and dive beneath the serene questioning of his lord and master which he knew was just about to follow. Bailey was wearing his gentle, inquisitorial air, and it was he who had suggested the drink. But drink made no difference. Whatever Bailey consumed never seemed to touch the sides, one of many reasons to admire him. And Ryan liked Bailey, respected him above all others, which was not saying much but was still considerable, although the liking was tinged with the reserve he would always have for indecently naked intellect and a copper who actually lived with a brief. Such a union was, as Bailey's Helen had put it, rather like a Montague actually joining a Capulet, placing Bailey even further outside the ranks of his own than he had been before, and her further still. Neither seemed concerned and Ryan envied them.

Cheshire's Wine Bar was all plants and bent-wood chairs, subtly uncomfortable. The young barristers went there to see their friends, and to be seen; the older ones hovered round the edges. Police officers were a rare phenomenon against the painted woodwork, and all the tables wobbled. Get on with it, Ryan asked his companion silently. For once, he wanted to go home. Whatever Bailey was going to ask, he knew he wasn't going to like it.

'I was wondering how you were getting on with Tysall.'

Oh, oh . . . No beating about the bush then, no how's your father and the kids: straight for the jugular. Feign honesty.

'Bloody awful. I told you what Simeon Churcher QC said,

didn't I? Can't find any more angles for now. I mean, except for the fact that he steals ideas and makes people bankrupt, appears to manage a brothel in that hotel of his, may have left the Stock Exchange before they caught him for insider-dealing, certainly steals from the taxman and trades in stolen antiques, and probably murdered his wife, the man's as clean as a whistle.'

'I see. You've joined his fan club? Look, Ryan, I know I've given you free rein, but we are supposed to be investigating fraud. That's why this is a Fraud Squad, if you see what I mean. There's supposed to be some connection with fraud in our daily lives, if you understand me. So if Tysall's a hope-less case for a fraud charge, forgery, deception, anything you like, you're supposed to report any other suspicions you have to his local Division, and let them run with it. Fraud is what we do.'

Ryan fingered the glass, brushing the moisture from round the side in straight lines.

'Are you telling me to do that? Sir?'

'You would insist on being so bloody direct.' Bailey's smile always transformed his heavily lined face, and Ryan remem-bered on sight of it how much he liked the man.

' . . . And no, I'm not telling you to do, or not do, anything. I'm just telling you not to get caught with your toes on the corns of some DCI on Division. Do what you like, with that in mind, and remember I don't need to know about it pro-vided you're turning in a respectable amount of legwork on all the other cases. But it's limited to three months. That's all the time you have to find something. Is that clear?'

Ryan nodded. Bailey relaxed.

'Now you can tell me why you go into overdrive whenever Tysall's mentioned. I've never known you so keen. Come on, Ryan. Tell me something about the man I don't know.'

'You know most of it . . . Oh shit. Look who's here . . . Mr Cook, sir, coming over . . . He's seen us.'

'Yes,' said Bailey. 'I thought he might be here.' Rather than pull himself into the shadow, Ryan's instinct, Bailey was waving at Malcolm Cook, who forged a path to their corner. Ryan sighed. Sly old bastard. No accident avoiding the crowded pub, was it? Smoothly oiling us both in here, knowing bloody well he'd get old Malcolm into this conversation. Probably thinks I need educating, and need the restraining hand of the Crown Prosecution Service. Amid the prickle of resentment for Bailey's effortless manoeuvres and Cook's inevitable legal authority, Ryan nevertheless felt the stirrings of relief. He had been ploughing a lonely furrow after all, and the relief persisted even as the deliberate blankness of both his interrogators showed the prearrangement of the whole trap.

'Ryan was just telling me,' Bailey remarked, pouring wine for Malcolm and lager for the Sergeant with remarkable economy of movement on the small, wonky table which had come to rest, painfully, on Cook's muscular thigh, 'everything he knows about Charles Tysall.'

The 'everything' was stressed lightly. Ryan was in the middle, another subtle trick: he was the stockiest but smallest of the three, and it seemed best to admit defeat. It took a secretive man like Bailey to recognise another, and Ryan supposed Bailey had understood his own hesitation in talking to lawyers, even lawyers like Cook, and even lawyers on the same side, especially lawyers on the same side who had the power to stop you, but he'd thought Bailey might have forgotten all that, what with marrying one of them. Montague and Capulet indeed, posh stuff. Beauty and the Beast, more like.

'Everything I know about blue-eyed Tysall? Well, you can have it in one sentence. He's a bastard.'

'No, no,' protested Malcolm, laughing. 'He's innocent, like all those people in prison. But apart from making his own companies super-rich at the expense of making others go under to the tune of a dozen suicides? That's all you ever told me.'

'That's all you ever asked.' Ryan was still truculent.

'Ryan,' said Bailey delicately, 'thinks that Tysall has a lethal attraction for redheads. Not they to him necessarily, although that does seem to happen, but more the other way round. Ryan is very worried about Mrs Tysall, whoever, and wherever, she may be. Also other redheads. My Sergeant has a vested interest in redheads.' Annie, lovely Annie, had been a kind of ginger. Ryan shot Bailey a glance, half plea, half venom. Bailey shook his head. No, he agreed tacitly, they need not mention Annie. Not if Ryan behaved.

'Come on, Ryan. Drink up, and cough up.'

'I didn't know Tysall had a wife,' said Malcolm, thinking in a shocking moment of his own pipe-dream and shrugging it away.

'We don't think he has either,' said Ryan, finally admitting familiarity in the sudden desire to tell. 'Not any more.' Each took a strong pull of drink, and waited. Bailey knew how well Ryan could tell a story.

'Half of this is gossip, you know, but I used to work out of Kensington, three years ago, before Mr Bailey saved me from ruin.' He shot Bailey his best glance of wolfish friendliness, the look which had enraged so many prisoners and frightened not a few. Never touched them, sir, only smiled. '... And once upon a time, filthy rich Charles Tysall, getting better-looking all the time, the women said, moved into a mansion block opposite Harrods. Seen after that, when we raided a couple of clubs on a big gaming round-up, but not a gambler. Always with a redhead, who sat so close you'd think she was tied to him. Mrs Tysall, that was; very nice looking woman, real charmer. Same woman seen by me, as it happens, when I was ... out with this woman ...' No, don't say it was Annie, or talk about Tysall's personal revenge on his clumsy pursuer, seen as clearly as his own observation. 'Well, never mind what I was doing, but I saw her in this club, with a man who was not Mr Tysall, her lawfully-wedded husband. I got the lads to keep a look-out: seems Mrs T might have been over the side, once or twice. Anyway, she paid for it. Came into Kensington nick looking as if she'd been hit by a bus, three times over a year. Once she told us he'd tried to rip out her fingernails, but she wouldn't show her hands to the divisional surgeon. Don't know what she wanted us to do about it, apart from give her shelter until he'd calmed down, because she'd never make a statement, and she'd never charge him.'

Ryan sat back, brow puckered with puzzlement. No woman in his own life had been so slow to accuse, but he never aimed to find out what they'd have done if he'd hit them. He still couldn't understand anyone wanting to try. It was the one piece of male unfairness he could not understand.

'Anyway, one day I took her back home, bleeding all over my new car. She had a lovely voice, Mrs T, and I asked her why she stayed with him. Because he loves me, she said. Funny way of showing it, I told her. He can't help it, she said. It's the way he is. If I try to go out, or look at anyone else, he goes wild, and it doesn't even take that. He doesn't like me thinking, even. Stop thinking out loud then, I told her, or he'll kill you, and as long as you won't bloody sign the sheet, we can't help. Oh no, she said. I'm sorry to trouble you, but it isn't so bad. He never scars me. The day he does that, I'll know he hates me. Then this tomcat will really have marked his territory, and I'll have to go. That was the time he'd broken her ribs. Why wait, I thought. Suit yourself, I thought. I wouldn't wait, not even for a pedigree tomcat. Which he is of course. Eton, Oxford, cultivated bastard.'

'He's not the only one around who thumps his wife,' Bailey said mildly, although his fists were clenched on the table. Ryan remembered the night when Helen West, Bailey's woman, had suffered at the hands of an intruder, and understood more of why his boss was giving him a freer rein than normal.

'Or she the only wife who refuses to take any action whenever she's roughed up,' Cook added. 'The wives withdraw the allegations. Good God,' he added with a grin, 'how do some men get away with it? If we tried any such thing, they'd be queueing up to murder us.'

114

'There's a difference here, sir. This wasn't a lout coming home from the pub and knocking his punch bag round the kitchen. This is a bloke who quite likes refinement with it. Mrs T had been tied up and beaten. Obviously he'd threatened to cut her face or she wouldn't have mentioned it. She was terrified, only she wasn't going to make it easy for him by letting him go and hopping out of it herself.'

'A masochist maybe? Parlour games with a difference?'

'No, I didn't think that either. Wrong type.'

Bailey wondered. Ryan might have been a dogged detective, but he was an easy champion, not quick to spot perversion in a pretty face. The Superintendent knew how his Helen had been in the face of attack, brave, but with all the normal instincts to do anything rather than repeat it. Even, thank God, living with him. She would have gone to the ends of the earth to avoid the humiliation of physical assault, and so, were she entirely normal and as far from helpless as Ryan described, would Mrs Tysall. Mink coats were rarely that important to people who wanted to stay alive.

'Anyway,' Ryan continued, 'she disappeared, Mrs T. Clean went. Saw the light, you might say, and buggered off. But not before he'd had a good go at her, really chewed her up. She'd not been seen for three weeks. One of the uniformed lads checked every day with the caretaker and kept an eye on the comings and goings for me. No sign, no visits to the nick either, but a woman of her description, and there aren't many, had been in the Brompton Hospital casualty having twenty-five stitches put in her face. Even then she wasn't reasonable. Brought a bloody puppy inside with her.

It sat and howled outside the ward. No one could shift it. I got that from a nurse I know.'

Ryan paused, looked at Bailey.

'And guess who took her to the clinic? Not Tysall of course, never does his own tidying up, but good old Ted Plumb. Never thought Ted was a good bloke, but he was once a good copper. What a way to go. No way but down. Getting your own car bloodstained by the boss's wife, being left with a howling dog.'

'Ted Plumb was a bad case,' said Bailey. 'In case you didn't know,' he explained patiently to Malcolm, 'Ted Plumb was a DC in the Central Drugs Squad. Peddled drugs, used them once I think, but not now. He did a very good job bargaining with the Commissioner to get out of criminal charges. Threatened to take a few with him. Anyway, you can't judge Tysall through his employees, or them through him. Yes you can, now I think of it. Sorry, that's only a sideline. Go on, Ryan.'

'All right. As I was saying, the lady stayed to get embroidered, then took herself to a private clinic in Mayfair. Couldn't get more than that. Then pfft! Gone like a cloud of red smoke.'

'Why couldn't it be investigated? Or am I being naïve?' Malcolm asked.

'With respect, Malcolm, you are,' said Bailey. 'Ryan only got hold of the medical stuff by accident. No way of getting hold of the records officially. No doctor was going to reveal them without the patient's permission, and no patient to be found.'

'You could have got an order under the Police and Criminal

Evidence Act for privileged material if you could show reasonable suspicion of a serious crime,' Cook pointed out.

'Oh could we indeed? And then what? One set of medical records showing multiple facial injuries, one reluctant witness who'll say she fell downstairs if ever we found her, and one Charles Tysall, who'd have a very expensive lawyer, and not say anything? We could get the records, for what? We hadn't a victim, we hadn't a complainant, and no one even reported her missing. I think he killed her. Not then, later.'

There was silence at this. And had Annie in between, thought Ryan savagely. He looked at Bailey, grateful for the silence, then took up the tale, tired of the sound of his own voice and bored with his own anger.

'They had a place in Norfolk – you know, pukka country cottage by the sea, complete with dishwasher, very rural – and she was seen there three months later. We're talking about two years ago now, but only seen for a couple of days. Walking round the village like a zombie, grinning at people, with a face like a battlefield and one squint eye. Then gave the keys to neighbours, said Ta-ta, she was moving on. No car with her, all tidy. Then no trace.'

'Has the yearning husband expressed an interest?'

'No, and no one else either. American she was, no parents alive, no friends, and no one expressing anxiety. So I can't, or rather Division couldn't, investigate, could they? What power have we got? You have to have a complaint before you can do anything, and all we had was him complaining of harrassment from me. I was told to lay off, and then Mr Bailey asked for me in Fraud. Come any closer to Tysall and what do you find? A man bristling with writs, who says his wife has simply deserted him, and what business is it of ours?'

'I see your point,' said Malcolm. 'Not even reasonable suspicion of foul play, and you'd have to explain your information from the nurse. Not much fuel in that even, if she's seen alive three months later. But that doesn't entirely explain your passionate interest in Mr Tysall, Ryan. There's more, isn't there?'

Here Ryan hesitated. Bailey knew why, albeit vaguely, Malcolm not. But only Bailey knew the signs of his Sergeant struggling with empirical conclusions, and struggling even harder not to look silly. Ryan drained the lager, shook his large head, appealed to the ceiling for help, and waved his hands in frustration.

'I dunno. Redheads is what there is. Not just a disappeared, hacked-about wife, but redheads. All over the shop. Looking at Tysall's files, raiding Tysall's office, the companies he's made bankrupt, having a look at his hotel accounts, there's always a redhead jumping out of a corner at me like those pop-up cards you give to kids. He seems to surround himself with them, and then they up and go.

'Or are you just seeing redheads because you've got them on the brain?' asked Cook. 'My mother told me whenever she was pregnant, or even thinking of it, the streets used to be full of pregnant women . . .'

'Well, I'm not bloody pregnant. Or red-haired. Or female. And not quite daft either.' Malcolm could see he had not chosen the best parallel. He smiled an apology, and Ryan went on grudgingly.

'There must be plenty of redheads around, but our friend Tysall finds a high proportion of them. And some of them don't come to any good, and none of them have families. All those without families come to no good at Tysall's hands, let alone the world at large.'

'Like who, for instance?'

Bailey answered. 'The receptionist in his hotel. Seen on Tysall's arm, next seen looking the worse for wear. Leaves job abruptly. No complaint. No family, of course. The private secretary in his office. Starry-eyed, goes downhill slower. Heroin overdose but rescued with funny compression marks on the neck. Catatonic, that's the word, isn't it? Won't say anything. Then the bright girl from the computer company, very obviously seduced, bowled over by our Charles. Ditched when her usefulness was over. Committed suicide a few weeks ago, just as Ryan thought we might get something out of her. I don't know what they do for him, or what they have for him, but he seems to haunt redheads.'

'Or be haunted by them?'

'As if he was looking for someone. Or something. Then he throws them away, or deliberately hurts them. Sorry, when we say all this it sounds daft. Let's have another drink, what else can I say that makes sense?'

'No,' said Ryan. 'My shout, I'll go . . .'

Bailey placed a hand on Cook's arm, a gesture to prevent him from insisting otherwise. If Ryan was embarrassed by his tale of woe, let him buy the round, make himself feel better and sink the dying vision of Annie.

'Hardly enough for a search warrant, is it, Malcolm? Or even enough to approach the Crown Prosecution Service with the idea of an official investigation?'

'Official, no, but continued unofficial investigation with a modicum of surveillance . . . '

'Yes, I'd say that, but you never heard me say it. The Met Police solicitors are the ones you should ask, but I know what they'll say, and if it's a second opinion you wanted, there it is. I'm only a senior principal. You know I can't give you any kind of real authority, and no one else would give it either. But I'll keep an eye on Ryan if you like. We've several other cases together already.'

'Good. That's all I wanted. He'll hate it, he hates being watched.'

'Well, I won't be watching closely. Simply the odd question here and there, and I'll take him out for a drink. It always makes him expansive. He likes me as well as anyone, I think.'

'Kind of you. Leave it there.'

Ryan was relieved to return to the table and find them discussing no more than mutual acquaintances, Bailey issuing invitations to his home. Since the past but still clearly remembered days of fatness, Malcolm's confidence had been so altered, he could not bring himself to court invitation, preferred his own company. Bailey was simply reminding him of an open door. Malcolm grinned at Ryan as Bailey left them both for home. He too had realised how many strands, how many benign purposes there had been in Bailey's skilful arrangement of the evening.

'Crafty blighter. Great bloke,' was Malcolm's grudging

contribution. They both laughed. As usual, Ryan's glass was empty.

'Don't know about you, Mr Cook, but it's like the other night. I've got the taste now, if you see what I mean. For talking and drinking, not sure which order. But not here. Can't go home early, terrible waste of a free evening. The wife's out.'

'Well, I'm going home. You come too, it's only a mile. See how the other half live.'

Ryan looked up in surprise. Friendliness from a lawyer was one thing, appreciated and mistrusted in equal proportions, even if you got drunk with them sometimes; but being invited across the portals of their precious houses was quite another, a rare occurrence, except perhaps between bent copper and dodgy brief. And yes, he would like to see how an honest one lived, and yes he did see there was something in the gesture which should make him wary. No one in Ryan's book, not even Mr Cook, gave something for nothing, but he would suspend judgement on that, for the moment.

Two hours later, Ryan left and returned to Cook's attic-flat laden with the Chinese food they had ordered. Conversation was flowing, freely. Ryan was finding a liking for wine. Cook could make him like the stuff, none of this poncing about with sniffing corks and that, and Ryan was even enjoying the prospect of being able to tell his wife. Most interesting evenings in Ryan's life could not afford that kind of follow-up, but he could tell her all about the visit, if not the conversation, thinking as he shambled up the street with the hot bag how odd it was that people like Malcolm Cook should

121

celebrate their modest and educated success by going to live in draughty old houses. Nothing so strange as folk. Thinking hard on that phenomenon and others, when he stopped, and almost released his hold on the carrier.

There she bloody was. Mrs Charles Tysall to the life, tripping down the steps from the big front door into Malcolm's house, collar turned up against the evening chill, exquisitely, formally dressed, as if for work, with a flow of red curls catching the light from the taxi-meter as she bent towards the window. Mrs Tysall had caught his fancy more than he had told, and Ryan's heart stopped, until he saw the clean lines of that smiling profile, so close he could almost have touched, and heard the voice giving pleasant directions. 'Gray's Inn, please.' Sarah Fortune, off to meet yet another lawyer. No, not Mrs Tysall, he saw with enormous relief and some regret. Just her double, without her gravelly voice or cut face. Not quite her height, but near as dammit, and his heart lurched into movement again, along with his feet, as the taxi pulled away, cheerful island of light in a dark street, diesel engine thumping. What a cracker, though. Thank God she wasn't Mrs T, he'd have looked a real fool saying hallo. And why did such silly objections occur to him? He would have preferred her to be found. And thank God, whoever she was, she lived the other end of London from good old Charles: she was just his type. And he'd have to ask Cook if he kept a fancy woman downstairs. No sign of anything like that in residence with the prosecutor. He'd looked.

'You've gone pale,' said Cook indoors. 'Was it the wine, or

the effort of getting to the corner?' Remarks had been made earlier on the subject of Ryan's small paunch.

'Do you know the neighbours, Malcolm?' First names were suddenly permissible here; when next met in court or office, Malcolm knew he would become Mr Cook, but for now he saw an easing. 'Only there's a right smasher just come out downstairs. Redhead. Thought you might be keeping something from me.'

'Don't know any of the neighbours. I haven't lived here long. Keep my head down, so do they. Perhaps I shouldn't.'

'Come on, Malc, you're kidding me. You couldn't have missed that one unless you're blind.'

'Well, I am, a bit. We all keep different hours, and when I go out, I go out to run.'

'Where does the girlfriend live, then?' Ryan asked, super-casual, ripping the foil-top from egg fried rice, sniffing appreciation.

'What girlfriend?' said Malcolm mildly, fetching plates to his fine polished dining-table, regarding his vegetable dish and Ryan's spring-rolls with something like resignation.

'Oh, come on, you don't look like a hermit. Not now you're so bloody slim. Where do you hide her?'

'Nowhere. There isn't one.'

'Well, stone me, you poor sod. I'm no advert for marriage, but I like to go home to someone, nice warm lapful.' He coughed, not wanting to repeat too much of the chequered Ryan history which at least gave him licence to lecture on the subject of women, but not to advise. 'And I couldn't be without the kids.'

'How many?'

'Two. Bloody babies, but the fact I've had two means Bailey at long last asks for my expert opinion on how to produce them, and that's a turn up for the books, I can tell you. No girlfriend, Malc? What's wrong with you?'

'Nothing. I just don't try. Well, I do, but not very hard. They're all so normal, the ones I meet. I'll take one out, sit down with her, then I think of this girl I met once, and I lose interest. Stupid, really. Can't ever get her out of my mind.'

Ryan wondered. He'd been that kind of dreamer once, not so very long ago, still dreamt of Annie before he'd had the sense to go home and Tysall had finished it all. Broken his heart. Only it hadn't quite put him off his stroke somehow. You might be with one of them wishing she was the other, but you still managed to do what a man has to do.

'Bit special, was she?' he asked with the sudden sympathy of fellow feeling.

'Yes, I suppose she was.'

'How long ago?'

'Don't know. About two years.'

'But look here, Malc, it won't bloody do, you know. How old are you, thirty-twoish? Two bloody years. That's a cop-out. You can't wait for everything to come right, you've got to get on with it. She'll be married to some other bloke by now. If she wasn't then.' So Ryan told himself firmly about the love of his life, every day. 'What you holding the torch for? Stupidity, don't want to get involved, some kind of loyalty, or what?'

'Not loyalty. Just hope might find her again, though I never did know where she lived, and she didn't want me to ask. More a question of making comparisons, and no one else compares. She was . . . very kind.'

'Well, stuff it. Find another one. The best ones never come back. I'm not saying they're all the same, but there's plenty as nice as one another. You can have my wife for four days a week. The other two she's mine, and on Sundays she goes to her mother's.'

Malcolm laughed, ate. 'Perhaps I've just lost my touch. If I ever had one.'

'Well, you can come out on the town with me. I'll show you where to find them.' It was an empty invitation: both knew they would do nothing of the kind, any more than Ryan would ever choose to live in a flat rather than a house, but the gesture counted for something. Ryan ate companionably, wondering why Cook liked so many paintings and plants. Perhaps the walls were bad, something to do with damp, but he had to admit it was restful.

'You know PC Smith at Clerkenwell nick?' Cook nodded. 'He told me this good story. Roughly about women. About a man from Yorkshire, the only one who could ride the famous donkey on the beach . . . You know the one?'

'Which famous donkey?'

'The one no one else could ride, vicious brute. Bucked and reared, and reared and bucked, and no one could stay on its back. Thousands of blokes on the sands tried every year, all failed, knocked off, ground into the sand, trampled by the dozen. Until this Yorkshire bloke, he stayed there, gripped on like glue, nothing could shift him. So they all stopped and

125

cheered and said, How do you do it, how do you do it, you've got to tell us . . . And he said, It's nothing lads, nothing, and they ask again. Where did you get the knack, tell us? And he says, It's nothing lads, really. I've allus been the same since the wife had whooping cough.'

Malcolm spluttered into his black beans while Ryan roared at his own story. Healthy attitude to sex is what Malcolm needed; apart from that he was pretty normal really, for a solicitor. He'd have to be to rise to that story. The wife hadn't liked it much. Nor had that social worker he'd told yesterday. Ryan's little test of humour showed he was happy.

One hour after, chirpy and dutiful, he went home for the train. Plenty to tell with a clear conscience, glad it was only midnight and also that, in comparison to Mr Cook's funny flat and empty bed, his own life seemed rosier. As he left, Ryan glanced at the front door of the huge old house, and the lit windows of the second floor, wondering which were hers. Nice to spot that redhead again. He may have been well-behaved these days, but there was never any harm in looking.

CHAPTER EIGHT

It was raining and dark after Ryan had gone, and Malcolm had the overwhelming desire to speak to his father. In case that wise old bird would extend into the vacuum some hint of affection, or even suggest he might know what to do with a financier like Charles Tysall. But no. To speak to his father was to try and speak a new language, and only ever served to renew the old quarrel. Perhaps at the Gray's Inn Ball, that grand annual occasion which both of them were bound to attend, out of long habit and his mother's insistence. Perhaps then, when they were both bound to be jolly, but not now. All Father would do now was scold, like an otherwise fair school prefect on a bad day, raise his voice out of the stiff collar of his outraged pride. Lowly public servant, he would yell, as he had yelled before. Struggling in the gutter for your trade, hardly like a proper solicitor, and probably damaged in the process. You fool. Yes, yes, Malcolm had said, all that and more. Exploited, bemused, saddened and maddened, usually on the losing side. You never change anything by prosecuting people, Father had shouted. No you don't, Malcolm had agreed, but then nothing changes people except luck, and at least this way I have the chance to protect the victims, that's the point. Besides, I get to laugh sometimes, which is more than you seem to do. But only sometimes. Not a dignified way of earning money, but my own, you see.

No, he would not speak to his father, however much he loved him. Tomorrow he would make ten more telephone calls in the search for Sarah Fortune; maybe he would succeed. She might have been a stranger, but he never lost the urge to talk to her again, or the belief that she would understand him. He had tried to will it away as he would have tried to deny the existence of a toothache, with the same lack of success for an ache which grew. The thoughts were jumbled: Sarah, Charles Tysall and his own father, all somehow ill-fated.

He could not bring hope of a prodigal return to his father, nor could he defend himself. If neither Ryan, Bailey nor himself could even draw the barge of the judicial system alongside Charles Tysall's yacht, then Stepfather would be proved right. Even if he were interested in criminal affairs, which Malcolm doubted, he never had, as far as Malcolm knew, encountered violence. Instead of speaking, Malcolm resorted to his old friend, the night. He went out like a burglar at midnight, ignoring the summer rain. Padding his dark route on shiny warm streets, looking for the man and the dog, wanting something to rescue.

There they were, on cue for inspection, the dog thinner than before, ratlike with damp fur, dragged each inch of the way, not even whimpering protest, while the man shrugged on, fighting his private battle with the world. Malcolm passed them once, then twice, sizing the frame of both, looking for witnesses. Then circled the block and ran from behind, silent, full of trepidation. Stealing was far from easy. He had begun to think like a thief, but was not a thief whatever his sympathies. May have watched it, read of it, but never embarked at dead of night with real theft in mind. Whether the kidnap was of handbag, child or animal, there was still a violence in it he could feel as he gathered speed, accelerating for the task, rushed softly to the man, snapped the lead from his hand, lifted the dog into his arms and ran on, panting in a spasm of relief before he reached the end of the street. There he stopped and turned briefly. The man was watching, passive but confused, arms by his sides in resignation, gesturing nothing at all, swaying slightly. Without the whimpering dog in his arms, almost weightless through long deprivation, Malcolm might have returned. He knew this one sad man would not change, not ever or not soon enough, neither for RSPCA inspectors nor anyone else. Malcolm's role in life left him no belief whatever in authorities: nothing was ever altered except by individual will. It was one of the reasons why he respected thieves. 'Got you,' he murmured to the dog. 'Why did I take so long? You might have died.'

They jogged home, two miles before the weight began to tell. No protest from the animal, plenty from Malcolm's limbs as he carried his damp bundle upstairs, and closed his door behind them. Once released, the dog, who appeared on closer inspection to be half spaniel, half nondescript, placed her matted rump on the kitchen floor, and regarded him with caution, her neck rubbed raw of hair and her eyes still bleary. Malcolm found eggs and milk, remembering gentle puppy diets. She wolfed food, eyeing him nervously as she ate, in case he should regret such generosity. Then the two of them, both thin animals used to greater quantities of flesh, examined one another with some hesitation and mutual admiration, like a couple of lovers still uncertain of the affair on which they were due to embark. In the end, they removed to the bathroom, where he washed the dog gently and towelled her dry, a treatment she disliked but did not resent. He had thought of a hairdryer to complete the process, abandoned the idea for fear the noise would alarm her. Still perplexed, he led her into the living room and sat in his armchair, admiring his handiwork. She sat on the carpet, looking at him again expectantly, and, after the briefest of pauses, crawled weakly into the capacious seat beside him. Acquired in his larger days, it held them both easily. She padded and snuffled damply, until they were comfortable.

Later he took her into the garden behind the house, found she did not try to escape but followed him back. He was adopting the same principle with the dog as he would these days with a kept-witness: if you wish to ignore safety and go home to violence, I cannot make you stay, though I wish I could. They resumed the chair by common consent. Together, they were seen by a dawn trickling through neglected curtains over the bodies of both which twitched and dozed in profound contentment. If it was a love affair, it was committed to continuance by the morning. In the course of the night, Malcolm's dizzy world returned to its own axis.

Ted Plumb's highly disturbed world was even worse than it had been. No matter if he forgot to feed it, or if the wretched creature was a nuisance he disliked, it had still been his dog. His by default, and the property of no one else. As he sat outside Sarah Fortune's house, not suspecting the presence of the sickly animal indoors on the top floor, Ted's loss rankled. He pulled the half-bottle from his top pocket. Two hours since the last drink, may as well be at work if you can't sleep at two a.m., and looking at this building was work of a kind. The liquid was fiery in his throat, nothing like the initial gulp, the sheer warmth of it, wish it didn't mean he would have to finish whatever was left in the bottle. That was the problem, never a single sip, never stopping at the stage when it was merely comforting.

He must not think of the dog, hadn't wanted it, and did not really want it now. Elisabeth Tysall's puppy. God, she had loved that thing, cuddled it like a baby, then, daft bitch, it had been left to Ted to kill it. He could not do so, but could not love it either. The dog had not wanted to stay with him, cried for its mistress night after night, always searched for her whenever they went out month after month. Same penchant for red-haired women as its master. He had tried to give the dog to the kids, they had not wanted it either, and now some bugger had stolen it. However mean the relationship, Ted had not wanted the dog stolen from him. There were enough humiliations without that. Made him weak, standing there like a pansy for some tall, thin bloke to snatch it out of his hands and run away. A reminder of the fact that he himself was incapable of running, incapable of protecting his own. His own hadn't wanted the dog either.

Tears of self-pity gathered in Ted's eyes. He took another mouthful, shook his head. Bugger the dog and let it rot, as well as the thief who took her. Look at the house first, where Sarah Whatsh-ername lived, whoever she was. Then go home, sleep and think, Good riddance. But first, concentrate.

Buildings had once been an interest of his, in the days when he had interests. A very large house, semi-detached, late-Victorian he guessed, flanking a small park, nice and quiet. One huge front door in the middle, two side doors either end; must be like a warren inside. Old houses like that would have had two staircases each side, one for family, one for the servants. Ted supposed they'd kept both. The flats on the top floor could use one side staircase each, or the main one if they chose; same for the second floor, but the grander flats on the first would probably ignore the narrower access. A sympathetic conversion, needing a coat of paint, but otherwise fine.

Ted was pleased, even for the damp summer warmth. Not unpleasant really, sitting on the bench in the small park opposite, quite pretty and peaceful, not the way it used to be, all teeming tenements at the back and faded splendour facing out bravely, neither poor nor quite rich. Respectable, he would call it, almost, but not quite grand.

Find out which flat she has, those were his instructions, or

132

what he suspected were only the first part of those instructions. How long was he supposed to watch, he'd wondered, but had not asked. As long as it takes, of course, is what Charles Tysall would have answered. She'd been out till after midnight, came back through the big front door, then the lights had come on in a second-floor flat, left of the door. He'd watched two others go in, side entrance right, wondering who else was in residence here, not that it was worth reporting. He had stayed as he was until all the lights were out, then gone to see if he could check names on the door. No chance, entryphone systems on all doors, occupants identified by number only, a trick to make them feel safer, though the doors themselves were as vulnerable as any other. Never mind. There were eight flats: someone was bound to lose a key sometime. Ted knew what estate agents were, he'd worked for one once before someone had spotted him. Down one end of the building was a For Sale sign, 'Luxury garden flat. Two Bdrms', the obvious way to get a key, but if a key was what Mr Tysall wanted, he could get it himself. Since Tysall had the looks to con himself into anything, getting a key from an estate agent was hardly an unsuitable task.

'*Pas de problème*, old son, but you've got to find yourself an informant. Someone who knows her. Someone who can give me an inside clue what she does with her life. Need a starting point. Can't do this all on my own,' Ted murmured to himself, hands in pockets, looking for the last cigarette. That was the trouble with observations, you smoked too much, as well as drank. Shambling away from the scene, he was vaguely bothered by questions, like what did Tysall want? But the curiosity was soon dismissed: all that was not his business. Ted's police career, abruptly and disgracefully ended, had accustomed him to obedience and a 'do now, think later' routine perfected into fine art. He was as grateful to Tysall as he could be to any man for the regular employment. Pity about Miss Steepel, pity about Maria and the others, pity about Mrs Tysall, but none of it was his business and nothing bore his fingerprints. And when Tysall crashed, as Tysall would one day, there might be pickings in plenty for himself, Maria and Joan, who might welcome him back with a fistful of cash. Ted would wait. There were always fortunes to be found in ruins, rings on broken fingers.

Watch what she does, he'd been told. I want a picture of her life. He was used to that too, the painting of verbal portraits. A few weeks should do it, allowing for some invention. Nothing difficult for a Drugs Squad man. Even one who could not keep a dog.

Soft-shoed Ted left no footprints. In the morning light, everything was normal. She could tell herself, speaking to the slightly dusty mirror in the hall, that everything was straight, and everything in place. The hall mirror, very old, fine and slightly crooked, gave a focus to her flat, revealing to her a simultaneous glimpse of the two rooms flanking it as soon as she came through her door. Squinting into it now, she could see that order reigned, or as much order as ever was in her own home. Sitting in the sunny kitchen, Sarah entertained herself to a mental review, uncomfortable, but necessary, before she could face the office and everyone in it.

Joan nagging more than ever, Ernest with his worried ulcer face, and all those life-histories from the corner shop to the reception desk of where she worked. Damn. Why did it all have to be so complicated when she had tried to make it so simple? She had run out of coffee, sugar and milk, wondered if it was sinful to eat chocolate for breakfast in the absence of anything else, thinking at the same time that she had a very strange notion of sin to consider it at all.

Everything was in its place in her complicated life, difficult but not impossible. No malice anywhere, generosity given from all her huge reserves, and received wherever she trod her diplomatic way, so why this unease? Charles Tysall was why. She was thinking of all her clients on the way to work, simply to remind herself of the comparisons of what had become standard in her life, and what was not, wondering if close knowledge of too many of the breed had weakened her imagination. Charles had ridden into her office like a god all those months ago, and no one but Sarah had been immune to his charm, and not even herself, at first. Stuffed in the perspiring crowds of the morning tube, she could only recall him with a shiver of frost.

'He's something special, Sarah. No kidding, promise.' Joan's breathless recommendation had been startling. Usually she was so scrupulous, so unimpressed by any client, however rich, who happened to cross the portals of the practice. Straggly Joan, so completely contemptuous of male charm, had been bowled over by Charles Tysall. Asked by Matthewson's secretary to take the man to Miss Fortune, she had embarked with ill-grace and mutterings. Stupid client insisting on seeing someone, having called in without appointment to see Ernest on a day off with the ulcer – his bad luck, wasn't it? Tell him to . . . Ernest had been the Tysall solicitor over many years, but since the firm must appear to pull together, and Miss Fortune was so good at placating people, she could take instructions, surely, whatever they were. She might not know any law, but she did seem to know how to please people.

'Why me?' Sarah had protested. 'Don't know him, don't want to know him, give him to one of the Commercial boys.' 'OK.' Joan raised her thin hands. 'I'll try and head him off.' Instead she had whistled back. 'You'll bloody well see him, gal,' she hissed. 'And if you think I'm taking someone who looks like a cross between Michael York and Omar Sharif to see one of those faceless little buggers in Commercial, you've got another think coming. 'Shut up, and comb your hair.'

So, Sarah had seen him. No, nothing urgent, he said. If ever there was, he'd forgotten. It could wait for the next day, but since he had been informed that she was more generalist than specialist, he had taken the opportunity of seeing her for a little advice on Industrial law. Could she help? She wondered wryly if he meant the same thing by 'generalist' as she did, and smiled at the thought since she could not see this man willingly consulting such a bodger of all legal trades, expert in none but vivid invention. Industrial tribunals were part of Sarah's mixed-bag of legal tricks, along with divorces and domestic upset, the 'also rans' of litigation. She had somehow found a role in the firm which was the provision of the sort of advice which no self-respecting

136

Commercial solicitor could touch with a long spoon, and hers was the loophole in the practice designed to prevent their clients going elsewhere, forming other loyalties in humbler streets. In any event, it did not matter how she came to be sitting in her untidy office with immaculate Charles Tysall on a January morning, while Joan fluttered in with coffee in borrowed china cups, lipstick-free. Sarah shot her a glance of amused suspicion, and Joan, scowling in response, almost patted the well-groomed head of Charles on her way past.

Powerful certainly, leonine and handsome: he was all of those. Also urbane, amusing and apparently modest, twinkling like a star with the pleasure and success of his life, and bristling with animal attraction. No one, thought Sarah, should have so much of it. They had achieved little in the meeting, except to agree what should be done with the dishonest employee, who Sarah suspected was no more than a polite device to hide the fact he was wasting her time, since he could not, or would not, speak of the real purpose of his visit, reserved for Matthewson's ears only. Then Charles Tysall had suggested dinner the same evening, and under the spell of very brilliant eyes, she had agreed and wished she had not. Attracted, but profoundly disturbed, dreading and looking forward without knowing why, feeling like a silly girl.

Meeting a strange man by arrangement in a strange place, a wine bar, was always an intimidation which none of Sarah's sophistication could quite dispel, but by the time she had arrived, she had given her mental defences a complete overhaul. Certainly Charles Tysall was a devastating man (she could only think of him, as Joan did, by resorting to teenage epithets), but with all the advanced instincts of her being, she knew he was an abnormal one, without pausing to define why. He was certainly not a potential client, nor a lover, nor a friend; friend least of all. She was early, willed herself into insouciance, ordered her wine, and, in the light and calm of the early-evening trade, read a book. Charles was late. She had known he would be late: men like Charles did not sit and wait.

She forgot the man, forgot to look for him, concentrated on the book, used her talent for losing the sense of time and place. It was the first contrast he could see between this and other meetings, the first insult and the first fascination. There she was, sublimely unconscious of his existence, lost to him, sitting in a corner and smoking without the smallest concern for the image she made, half-way down a bottle of excellent wine, carelessly turning a page, profoundly content to exist, with or without his presence. She was not allowed such nonchalance, nor could he know how difficult it had been to achieve, but it was unnerving all the same, greeting a woman who looked as if it would not bother her in the least if he had simply failed to arrive.

So why did he try? He who hated wine bars, assignations, anything unpredictable and women in particular. Hated the way they shrank from him, or opened up like sea-anemones looking for prey, every orifice gaping greedily in a panoply of slack mouths, glistening for himself, or for any other. Docile animals on heat. Equally, he loathed the others of sly reserve, with their tongue-tied giggles, looking and preening, wobbly and silly in response to the worst flattery, voluble after the most bland curiosity, as tactile as waxy flowers. He despised as much the brittle wit which proved itself with funny faces, wisecracks, street wisdom and worldly knowledge displayed to show how wise, how sharp the speaker. Charles had met only one woman inside the last fifteen years of his own life who did not fall into one of these three categories, did not respond towards one of these extremes, adulation, stupidity, or competition. While he, chameleon that he was, would enter into the spirit of all roles, changing colour or changing skin, shivering beneath it all with sheer dislike of playing games with those less skilled. For what? The horror of the prospect of failure, not of going home alone (although he would often circle the block rather than enter his own abode after midnight: not dread, simply disappointment not to find anyone there). Whatever he had hoped to find for her replacement proved as elusive as ever. For more than two years he had been in pursuit, been offered, looked beneath stones, while sexual gratification was always provided by some willing Maria, some commercial body paid for humiliation. Desire, naked or otherwise, repelled him. Indifference or refusal, any controlled or hidden reaction, had an effect dramatically opposite. Charles liked to hunt, but if he lost, was crossed, ignored, or worse, humiliated, the fury and the violence were terrible in manifestations cold, sharp and calculating.

And there in the bar was the graven image of his wife, before she was disfigured, the woman he had sought for two years. Sarah Fortune could have been the double in feature, superior in wit, but the nose, the mouth, the shape, the walk,

139

all the same. Apart from that quality of innocence, there was a shining kindness in her intelligent face, which Charles mistook for his ideal of purity.

He remembered the last Porphyria. I love you, she had said. 'How much?' he had asked, wanting to know at first, later shouting at her. 'Surely you can do better than that; you do not love me enough to serve me . . . Tell me something I can believe . . .'

'Why should I, Charles? I'm only your prisoner, so I'll say, I love you, Charles, and you can believe it or not, as you wish. I'll say whatever you want me to say . . .'

And then he had hit her, hated her for all that endurance in her refusal to bend to his will. She had clawed back at him, screaming. He could not remember any pain, nor, as she had told him later behind her mask, had she.

> *No pain felt she;*
> *I am quite sure she felt no pain.*
> *Like a shut bud which holds a bee,*

So said Browning.

Here was the new Porphyria, his wife before he had marred her. She was not dead, had never left him after all.

'You are very beautiful,' he had told Sarah Fortune.

'For the compliment, thank you. I shall treasure it. Although it isn't true. I don't think I have that quality. Perhaps I'm lucky; well constructed, built to last. But not, I think, beautiful.'

'Are you always so pedantic?'

'No. A response to awkwardness, a lawyer's trick. A desire to be exact, and seen to be honest. Even in candlelight.'

'Why awkward? Do I embarrass you?'

'Yes, since you ask.'

'Why?'

'You are a man of singular attraction, and I am slightly afraid of you. I tend to be pedantic when wary, or weary. At the moment I'm suffering from both. You must forgive me.' She sipped her wine, and smiled.

Bizarre conversation, so easily slipping from pleasantry and into this disquieting intimacy so soon. And the scarred faces he saw in his dreams faded away into this cool unscarred mouth which told neither truth nor lies, showed humour but no deference, both open and closed. Only after he had circled the block, pressed open his own door, entered his cold house, did he notice how skilful she had been. He knew no more of her life, her history, her tastes, and more importantly, where she lived than he had known in the beginning. Unwilling perhaps, but this time he was better equipped for pursuit and all the rest would follow. A pursuit he would not confess to Ernest Matthewson, but still a pursuit of his pure ideal, the chase to be surreptitious and delicate in tune with the goal. He had dreamed of her daily. O my Porphyria. Perfectly pure and good.

Put him out of mind, Sarah thought, pounding up the steps from the tube. No one watches you, knows you, no one ever has. Don't ruin it all by being a fool. Nothing is getting worse. He may have kissed you once, but he has not rung that bloody phone in days. (She remembered the kiss, an expert pressing of himself into herself, knowing she was too polite to escape or show the squirming revulsion of her mouth.) He had taken the refusal as a sign of innocence – dear God, what an irony. But he did not, could not possibly know where she lived. No one knew that, unless she had asked for them to know. Safe, so she was. Safe as daylight. And late again. Joan took the telephone calls for Miss Fortune, worried and resentful. Some of the many men left names, some did not. Fred could not wait to see her. Pink Jade had lost in the four-thirty at Leicester but, as always, he had another, better horse, which would make their fortunes brighter.

CHAPTER NINE

In the darkness of north Norfolk, horribly still after the noise of his familiar suburb, Ryan heard a dog bark, snuggled back into his bed, and dozed, wondering how he should be so content. All this was his wife's idea, but just because he was so anxious to please her these days did not mean that Ryan was putty in her hands. The resistance to her wishes and whims might have been token, but it wouldn't have done to let her know how anxious he was, so he did his clever best to hide it. In turn, she was well aware of the anxiety and took a smug satisfaction in it. Serve him right: infidelity was a dangerous game and it was he who had taught her how to play. Ryan's telling himself that she was only taking her revenge, a preliminary, perhaps, to their still tenuous marriage settling into equal terms, did not make his life easier. Cold comfort was his own counsel, recognised for what it was as clearly as he could see that the new hairstyle, prettier clothes and trimmer figure were not for him, but for someone else. A man met in the afternoons and early evenings of life. Ryan, receiving payment in kind, was humbled by the knowledge. Anything she liked, as long as she did not abandon him into that homeless wasteland he had inhabited when he had temporarily abandoned her. So now, while she preened a little, ruled her roost with a firm hand, and positively encouraged him to stay out late in the evenings, Ryan held his tongue, took the small mercies of her scrupulous care of him, and agreed with all her plans.

No foreign holidays this year, she had said. What's wrong with England? Too much money gone on clothes and her new car, Ryan thought, and made a big show of nagging which was met with the iron will he had expected. Ryan did not give a damn where they went. Family holidays were his idea of hell and a fisherman's cottage on the Norfolk coast struck him as a singularly unpleasant alternative, but after he had looked at a map and read a book of words, she had seen him become suspiciously resigned. He had learned that the place where they were bound boasted a pub which sold the best bitter in the world, and five miles away was Merton-on-Sea, the village and tiny port where Elisabeth Tysall was last seen. Busman's holiday, maybe a little scouting over the dunes, the thought of it obscurely cheering. Ryan laughed at the thought of himself as country detective; he had never spent more than a day or two out of the city, but especially in the context of his uneasy family life, the sniff of Tysall was enough to resign him to the packing, although it might not be enough to ensure a week of harmony. His was not that kind of family.

Ryan's boys were nine and six, and through all the hours when they drove him to distraction he loved them more than the world, and willingly accepted the wisdom of his wife's holiday decision when he saw them rushing in and out of the small, square cottage she had found. The dreadful details of the place dismayed him: the lack of light, the tired-looking beds, thin curtains and cold thick walls, but he could see it was all the details which so captured his children. They were howling with excitement. 'Dad! The garden's full of nettles, and there's a shed, Dad, with a door hanging off and all spiders inside . . . ' 'Dad! There's a ditch at the front with frogs and newts, and my blanket's got holes, Dad, look . . . '

Wonderful, thought Ryan. Fucking marvellous.

But something was there which charmed him by the end of the third day, when the silence of the place had ceased to alarm him and the strange creeks creeping inwards from the sea no longer preyed on his nerves. They had actually, in the absence of any other entertainment, swum in sharp frozen bursts, with the wife neat and blue-skinned in a new bikini, which Ryan noticed even between chattering teeth, liking the idea that for the first time in six months he knew where she was for every minute of the day. She seemed to like it too; their double bed was soft and sagging, so they rolled into the middle, gratefully sleepy with fresher air, but not that sleepy. Comfortable love and talking, surprising chatter for a man of so few words in his own house. By instinct, Ryan knew better than to force the pace of this intimacy by asking questions in those quiet and sympathetic hours. Nothing would have wrecked the harmony more effectively than him saying, 'All

145

right, who is he, this other bloke?' So he stroked her reddish hair instead, told her all about Tysall, with some notable omissions which they could never discuss, and persuaded her to spend a day in Merton-on-Sea. With a couple of hours off for him to amble into the local nick and see if anyone had heard of a certain missing lady whom no one else believed was dead. The wife was as full of new wisdom as Ryan. This domestic peace, this actual confiding in her of something to do with his work, was well worth the sacrifice. She and the kids would find a boat. Ryan could wander at will, and would miss them immediately.

He found the local bobby on the quay, gossiping and laughing with housewives, difficult to sound at first, calmly suspicious next. But prejudice against a confessed member of the Metropolitan Police, renowned to rural forces as being overpaid, over-corrupted, arrogant and flash, had not fully permeated into the mind of PC Curl, who simply liked people and had a position in his own community tantamount to the local vicar, only more important. He was easily persuaded by Ryan's open face which was flushed out of city pallor by three days of gusty sun.

'Not official, you say? Mr Ryan, you say? Elisabeth Tysall? Oh yes, went off to America, didn't she? They had a house, up there ...' He waved uphill, away from the quay. 'Had an accident, she did. So she said, 'bout two year ago. Used to come here three or four times a year. Very nice lady, very polite.'

'Did they know many people here?'

'Not so's you'd notice. Not him anyway, but she'd talk

to anyone. But it's a crying shame that house being empty. Plenty of young folk around here could use that house.'

Ryan listened, trotting beside the long length of PC Curl, laughing and praising, comparing lives. Finally, still talking of anything else but Mrs Tysall, they turned into the tiny police station on top of the rise.

'Open every day we are, in summer that is,' said PC Curl, proudly. 'No call for us much in winter. They have to go to Fakenham and report their missing dogs.'

The man's placidity was wearing, and Ryan envied the kids out on a fishing trip. They'd be full of it, he longed for them, while over a steaming mug of tea he was almost trusted.

'Now see here.' Even his voice was changing, developing the local speed. 'There's no inquiry going on about this Mrs T. Just me happening to think that her disappearing is a bit funny. No one ever saw her again after she was down here early part of last summer. No trace. Never came back.'

Curl shook his head dumbly.

'Why should there be anything? She don't live here. She's living in London, with her husband or without him, let him worry. She had a little puppy second last time, but didn't bring it back. Probably got tired of it, wanted a string of babies, that one. Strange creatures, women. And she said in the shop she was going abroad, see.'

They both watched vapour rising from the tea.

'But,' here PC Curl chortled with remembered worry, 'my nephew in spring, after the high tides, he found her bank cards.'

Ryan gripped the mug, and let it go hurriedly. Too hot,

and the rest of him flushed with sudden heat from the fin-
gertips down, sipping slowly to save it becoming obvious.

'Bank cards?'

'Yup. Them things, Access and Barclay. Can't like them
myself. They get people into all sorts of trouble. But they
don't perish in the sea. Most things do.'

'Did you report the finding?'

'Nope. Why should I? Checked with the bank places, all
computers, Access and Barclay. Discontinued, they said,
not lost or stolen, nothing else for me to do. She should
have handed them back, they said, if she didn't want them
anymore, but she probably just chucked them off the quay.
People are always chucking things off the quay. They don't
realise how they come back, eventually. Might take a year or
two, but they usually come back.'

'Where did the boy find them?'

'Out in the channels, stuck in the sand-banks, down a
hole, he said. Little bugger used to be frightened of the water,
now he can't get enough of it. Loves them creeks, ever since
his dad got him a dog. Walks up there at low tide. Always
bringing me things. Tell you what, he's not at school today.
I'll call him in. He'd like to meet a copper from London.
Make his day for him, but you'd better look fierce. Only lives
on the quay. He'll be home now. Tide's high. Nowhere for
him to go.'

When Ryan faced the boy in the bright daylight of the
front office where no one seemed to consult the police except
for a chat, he saw a golden child of spectacular thinness and
more freckles than he had ever noticed on a ten-year-old.

They had merged into a dark shadow over the bridge of his nose, making him look smeared, a permanently worried sand-boy. Quiet child, Ryan thought. Fit as a monkey, and, given the task of prizing secrets out of this little head, he would have felt more optimistic with a team of professional blaggers, each armed with a lawyer. Another half-hour, delicate questions unravelling from the child. Do all coppers in London carry guns? Has anyone ever had a go at the Crown Jewels, and if they did, how would they do it? And had the Queen ever come to where he worked? And where, at last, had he, over-polite boy, so different from Ryan's own, found the plastic cards belonging to Elisabeth Tysall?

'In the creeks, right out by the sea. You can walk all the way out there.' Well, fancy that. Did that mean they were actually dropped there? The child burst out laughing, pleased with superior knowledge. Oh no, it didn't mean that at all. They could have come from the quay, from a boat, or all the way from Brancaster, miles either side. The water, you see, takes things everywhere. No clue at all in where they were found, how silly of him.

'Anything else with the cards, was there?'

'No.' They had a pause of infinite length. 'But they had a piece of elastic keeping them together.' The mouth was firmly closed. 'I'd best go. Mum'll have tea ...'

'And so must I,' said Ryan. 'Or my wife'll kill me. Thanks for the afternoon. Come and see me in London.'

All suspicion lost in their final easy burst of goodbyes, uncle and nephew united in secrets and opinion. 'Oh no,' they said. 'Don't mean to be rude, but you wouldn't see me

149

dead in a place like that.' Ryan might as well have suggested a day in Valhalla, and he left them as he found them, courteous, closed strangers.

The boy had found the whole handbag trapped in the heather at the top of a bank. Or rather, his dog had found it, crazy puppy, new Dad's idea to reconcile him to life and his terror of the sea. A leather bag full of sand and wonder, half-chewed and stiff by the time he had rescued it by running half-way to the sea in pursuit. They might have taken away the puppy, or punished her, and the handbag was still in his own room, what was left of it. Good, salt-ridden leather. The dog was still chewing it. The coins in the purse had been tempting, but the sodden letters, tied up in cellophane like the parking-tickets his uncle gave to tourists, bits and pieces, rings, the purse itself, had all gone on Dad's bonfire. Only the niggling conscience, and the fear that they would not burn, had transferred the plastic things to his favourite uncle, with half story, half truth. Uncle had understood. They didn't want trouble, either of them.

Best friend to man and boy, Malcolm's dog wanted nothing but his existence. He had decided to call her Dog, a name of dignity he thought, because he would never be able to think of her as anything else, and she was, after all, the only dog in the world. She loved the windows of his flat, loved the park with the children and the grass made brown by football players and walking populace, thick with dirt and rich in smells. She had a remarkable penchant for following women and fawning on them, but most of all she adored Malcolm with a devotion bordering on the manic, and the sound of his step on the stairs provoked such an exhibition of frenzied affection they were left exhausted.

'Down, girl, down, you silly mutt. Get down ...' Vain requests against her panting enthusiasm and vapid attempts to reach his face. She was a kissing dog; she feinted and growled like a cat purring, great daft paws on his chest in ecstasy, only ready afterwards for a brief, unconvincing show of obedience.

Impossible to conduct a life of privacy with Dog, out of the question to resist her affection, or remember the frustrations of work in her company, and Malcolm felt a strange belief that this was the point from which he should begin his life afresh, and grow again. Any form of growth but size, he reflected wryly. Dog would bring him luck as he brought her health, but he wondered what he would do with her when he and his parents issued forth in the next week to go to the Ball. He hated the thought of excluding Dog from anything: the only time she suffered distress was from being left alone.

It was late afternoon when Malcolm looked beyond the dust of his office window, felt Dog hidden by his feet, and thought fleetingly of Detective Constable Ryan by the sea. Then he pulled towards himself, for the hundredth time, the Solicitor's Diary. Eight more calls to go in the daily hunt for Sarah Fortune. He had reached the M's in the directory, and found, startling in its familiarity, the name of his father's firm. It was a laughable thought that Sarah Fortune could be working so close to home. He almost abandoned the thought of making the call but, led by a sense of thoroughness, persisted. His voice, if not his mind, suddenly official.

'Hallo. I wonder if you could help me? My name is Malcolm Cook, solicitor. I was in the High Court last week and a lady in the case after me lent me a good pen, which I'm afraid I failed to return. I believe she was from your firm, but I'm not sure ... Do you have a solicitor, thirtyish, red-haired ...? I believe the first name was Sarah, but I didn't catch the rest. You'll inquire? Then I could return her pen. Thank you.'

Tapping his fingers while the faceless receptionist was busy with questions. 'Here, Sylvie, I've got this bloke asking for someone like Sarah, what do I say?' 'I dunno, put him through to Joan.'

Suspicious, but trained to be helpful. Usually, if a redhead existed within the walls of the office Malcolm was calling, he would be put on to herself or her secretary, and would know within seconds, by a mere detail of the voice or the description, that the trail was cold. This time it was a secretary with a voice breathing the fumes of a hundred cigarettes, and a manner as brusque as a sergeant.

'Sarah?' said the voice loudly. 'Sarah Fortune?'

There was a pause, whilst Malcolm held his breath, maintained the indifference of his tone, and listened with rising hope to the sharp intake of breath.

'There ain't no Sarah Fortune here,' said the voice abruptly. 'Our Miss Winfield has red hair, but she isn't called Fortune, and she's retiring soon. Never goes to the High Court anyway. Must be a different woman.'

'Thank you,' said Malcolm, spirits sinking. 'I'm sorry to have troubled you.'

Joan's hand trembled as she replaced the receiver. She had not acted in response to orders, only to instinct, an automatic reflex of protection and fear. If Sarah had noticed how subdued her secretary was these days, she had not commented. Knew better from past experience than to try to force Joan out of one of her depressive moods, finding it wiser to grin and wait for the storm to pass into healthier rage before deciding how to help by whatever back door she could find. But there was no help for Joan to seek from Sarah's generous source, not now. Before her eyes, on the other side of the desk, there lingered the vision of that small, broad man who had found her two weeks before in the office, and whose presence had reduced her to this. Deception and misery, cutting Joan off from all support, Ted's favourite and most effective practice.

She had shopped late one Thursday night, returned to the office reluctantly to finish some work, a rare enough occurrence and one she would never repeat again. Tapping up the corridor, suddenly awed by the hollowness of the quiet, she had heard him, sensed someone in Sarah's room. Sudden fear had melted into angry curiosity, and her thin shoulder had pushed the door open wide before she had given herself time to wonder who was this shuffler of paper, or even to consider that he might be sinister. There had been this squat man, with his hands in a drawer and his small feet below the desk, scruffier than when she had seen him last, but still dapper, if thinner and slightly dirty, looking up from his task with something like resignation, well-established in Sarah's chair.

''Ere, what the fuck do you think you're doing?' Joan's shrill cry rang futile in her own ears before the other instinct made her aware of danger. She stood still, unable to move from the circle of his untroubled gaze, shocked by recognition.

Ted Plumb recognised foe and friend, his mind calculating with speed as he moved towards Joan's paralysis, holding her eyes until he reached her, then pinning her arms and forcing her down into a chair. He had been in the office for over an hour, slipping in as the stragglers moved out, had seen the children's photos on Joan's desk, recognised Jack, knew for the first time where Joan worked, and had also surmised exactly how she stood in relation to Miss Fortune, whose desk had yielded a surprising set of secrets. There were angles in plenty here, levers and weaknesses for blackmail. Feeling Joan's arms begin to tremble, he knew he could afford to be almost honest, and was suddenly ashamed by the hunted look in her eyes. There she was, his informant.

''Allo, doll.'

His own shock had struck and passed when he had seen the photographs and recognised the detritus of his wife's familiar presence. A new bag on the floor, identical to the old, Joan's hat, Joan's bits and pieces in her desk, the lipstick which would always have that chewed appearance, the cheap cosmetics, the colourful scarf over the chair which he had touched in passing, smelt for sentiment, stopped in his tracks by half-regret. Yes, he missed her, more than he had known, wanted to be in those photos, a man with his kids and a careworn, but still striking wife. Better than a bedsit, a pile of dirty clothes and the occasional company of a foreign tart.

Joan struck at the arms holding her still, calmer but still rigid with shock.

'No need for that, Ted. Get your bleeding hands off me. And fuck off, I'm getting the caretaker.'

He sighed. Work was work, and this was far too important for other loyalties. Act first, make up the ground later. One slap to stop this effort to escape. A loud slap in the silence of the empty corridor, a reminder of her real isolation compared to his physical strength. One blow was enough, the rest was words.

'Come on, Joan love. Don't be silly.'

A red patch glowed crudely on one cheek. She did not respond. He pulled the chair from behind Sarah's desk and placed it next to hers.

'All right. Don't speak to me, but listen, will you? I'm not here to spy on you, didn't even know you were working here, how could I? You never tell me nothing, Joan, do you?'

Silence.

'Now listen, love. I've got this job. Charles Tysall, you know him?'

She did not reply, but he saw the flicker of awareness in her eyes.

'Poor bloke's in love, see? Like you and me once.' Not a good comparison, so he hurried on. 'Only she won't have nothing to do with him, your Miss Fortune, I mean. Nice woman, is she? Helps with the kids quite a lot, doesn't she? Thought she did. I seen her with Jack. Am I right?'

He held Joan's chin and shook it playfully. She nodded her reply.

'Now,' he continued, confident of her full attention. 'Now. All we want is what's best for Miss Fortune, what's best for you and the kids. Quite easy really. You just do as I say, simply speak nicely to Mr Tysall whenever he rings up, tell him what your lady boss is doing, and try to get her to speak to him if you can. Give him a chance, keep telling her what a good bloke he is. Don't let any other blokes she doesn't know speak to her either. That's all, and then no one gets hurt. Nothing to worry about. Nothing at all.'

Nothing. An empty building, the light above the desk illuminating dusk in early summer, washing out the workday sanity of the place. Not a sound, apart from his voice, even the street quiet outside. Joan had thought of her own rowdy estate, shrieks, howls and yells, sandwiches thrown to kids through the window, all that lovely, irritating noise. She had looked at the flat eyes in front of her own and known, without needing to reason, how captive he was. In those eyes, in her own street, in this room, prisoner day by day to all the loyalties and necessities. Ted and Sarah: threats to Sarah would threaten the whole of Joan's life. He knew it, and so did she. Children galloped through her mind; pictures of broken legs, burns, scars, and the emptiness of the place rendered her hopeless before Ted, as hopeless as she had always been when faced with a plea in his eyes. She had loved him, missed him, worthless bastard that he was.

She bent her long spine into the chair, a small gesture of defeat. Trembling, she reached for her bag, looking for the inevitable cigarette which might help her pretend defiance.

'Steady on, girl,' he said quietly and gently. 'I'll do that for you. Day's been long enough. Don't want to upset you, honest I don't.'

He had lit her one of his cigarettes, and the sudden kindness unhinged her frayed defences. Ted knew when to vary the strokes. She took the cigarette first, then the hand, then tolerated the arm round the back of the chair. It was a male arm, unlike Sarah's slender one, convincingly broad. Ted Plumb came from the same frightened place; they had shared too much of it together. It was all so much easier, so much more regrettable than he could have imagined, simply a question of finding by accident another loyal servant, full of weakness.

'It's very simple, see? But your Sarah, lovely woman, won't see sense. Don't know why. Sorry to rough you up, but you know what I mean. I've no business here. I'll come back in the morning if you like. But I need this job, Joan, really I do. He'll put me back on my feet. Good money, and then perhaps . . .'

She did not like. Even withdrawing from him, there was a spell, a mystical charm, Ted Plumb's fatter face transposed on the thinner, handsome face of his master. Whatever she thought in her mix of love and bitterness for Ted, she could not believe wrong of Charles, and she had simply agreed. Guard Miss Fortune, tell me, and tell Mr Tysall whatever she does. Save your husband from the scrap heap in the process, without doing any harm, simply doing Miss Fortune a big favour. Ted always had a way of dignifying a task, rendering betrayal a thing of worthwhile purpose. It was only afterwards Joan began to wonder, but even then she did as she had been told, telling herself it was all for the best, and such was the mixture of hope and reluctant loyalty, she believed it most of the time. Money, he had promised. Money and security after this, soon.

But today was a bad, fitful, trembling day when she knew it could not be so harmless. A strange man asking for Sarah, Sarah's very existence denied on an impulse. Joan lit another cigarette. Not only that. Bloody Charles Tysall's now familiar voice. What news for me, Joan my dear – a voice which caressed. Well, she's going out to lunch, on Saturday she's going to a ball. Where? Gray's Inn, something like that. She was talking about a dress. He had found something significant in that. She had tried to keep it brief since she could not see it was useful information at all. Felt all her resentments of Sarah and the world, all the reluctant respect, then put her head in her hands and wept.

CHAPTER TEN

Gray's Inn Ball, last word in effort on the Bar's social calendar of which Ryan and Malcolm had spied the first on Temple Lawns, the grandest ball for Cinderellas and Prince Charmings of all ages. Joan envied Sarah the Ball, Sarah dreaded it. There were too many memories, too many complications among all that glitter, and none of it was gold.

Reasons festered in several separate minds for hesitating. Matthewson, invited by Queen's Counsel as a gesture of thanks for all the expensive litigation brought to the fashionable door of chambers, hated the thought as much as Penelope loved it, and the loathing had driven the ulcer into a frenzy. Penelope wept with frustration at the defeat of her plans to reconcile father and son over the champagne. She and Malcolm would go to the Ball and make the best of it, she with her friends to meet him there. Malcolm placed Dog in his car, fingered his tie, and hoped it would rain.

Charles Tysall, non-practising barrister, had found it easy to organise an invitation through the old school contacts who would prostrate them-selves to please so successful a contemporary. He would find Sarah Fortune, trapped by politeness, unable to refuse to speak to him, or even be touched. So far he knew her instincts well, and dressed for the Ball with easy determination. Porphyria would suit an evening gown.

Sarah Fortune, poised in front of her mirror, ready for flight, wished for peace and the end of all perplexity, stuck out her tongue at her own image and wished it was a night for a long bath with frivolous book to consume during an evening of wilful inelegance. Wondered too what it was like not to be playing a part. Wished she could recapture excitement, and wished for more than a moment that someone loved her, even that hopeless love in a vacuum once held for a husband, never reciprocated, always denied, finally betrayed. And in the mirror, she still saw a dumpy child, permanently unloved, surprised by the verdict of the world's attention, begging not to go to the Ball. There in the glass was the reflection of an anxious face, the drawn look irritating her own observation. She hunched her shoulders, scowled at the result. Nothing was going to make her any the less recognisable, the blessing and curse of her own appearance ever since childhood. She could not have left her house with unwashed hair but the clean version shone like a bonfire however she pulled, scraped and twisted it into pins. Nothing could make her unnoticeable, however soberly dressed in this shroud of shapeless black, anonymous below the subdued hair. Maybe a pair of spectacles and a paper bag for the rest of the face would complete the disguise, she thought savagely, but even Simeon would notice that. God, this is going to be awful. Impatience rose in her throat in the form of a few gentle obscenities addressed to the mirror. Damn and blast. I never cared for opinion, good or bad, I will not pretend, I will not. Then the mirror reflected the same ironic smile, same lack of dutiful gratitude which had made Belinda Smythe recoil in surprise two years before. Sarah unbuttoned the high neck fastening with one hand, began to release the hairpins with the other. Hair undone, dress at feet, she pulled from the wardrobe a very different garment of cardinal purple, soft and shimmering, pinched at the waist, flounced at the bare shoulder, still demure, but a dress of curves and vivid subtlety of colour. She left it on one side, went to the kitchen, poured a large gin, then shook her hair and threw away the hairbrush she had used to torture it, stepped into the dress and downed the drink in one. After that she stuffed keys, cigarettes, lipstick and cash into a bag, blew a kiss at the mirror and walked out of the flat into the last of the late evening sun. Striding over the grass towards the road, she resembled a hiker in her long-legged and determined stride, unimpeded by the dress which she held to the knees. Cigarette in hand, she waved down a taxi, failing to notice that three of them, together with one bus and a private car, all stopped in unison. Thank you. Gray's Inn, please. If I'm going to the Ball I'm going to the bloody Ball. Not creeping there.

Ten o'clock. Gray's Inn, in splendour for the evening, covering its elegant façades and squares in lights so much more entertaining than its daylight preoccupations allowed. Gray's Inn Fields, once a meadow, the past only betrayed by the present names, Jockey's Fields, Field Court, flanking Gray's Inn Square and South Square, both bordered with Georgian stone and gracious windows. Beyond these were the walks, one and a half acres of pristine lawns with bowed trees, the envy of top-deck bus passengers in the road beyond, who saw from their own captivity a sanctuary of peace railed and protected from the ordinary world. And now, with trees festooned with lights, the grass half-covered by huge marquees and a small fairground, all disguised with the final transformation completed by the entrance of hundreds of revellers in evening clothes. Pipe bands in the walks, orchestra on the marquee dance floor, alternative band in hall, casino in the library, jazz or films in the Arbitration room, dinner out of doors, breakfast in the refectory, and all survivors to assemble for photographs at four-thirty in the morning. High Court judges, Sarah, Mrs Matthewson and others hoped to be home before then.

Tables in one marquee, cramped and cheerful, a crowd as large as New Year in Trafalgar Square, Simeon in earnest conversation with the lady he hoped to impress, Sarah entertaining his guests, and all relatively well. Mrs Penelope Matthewson, instructing her son to replenish the wine supplies before the rigours of dancing, looked as happy as a child at Christmas, and Malcolm ran errands with good grace, pleased to please her for once. Until he stopped in his wide-angled glance across the vista of tables, shocked by the sight of Sarah Fortune, held out of touch by a sea of faces, delightfully familiar all the same. Forgot the wine, and forged towards her as the tables' parties began to break up and move on to other entertainments, obstructing his path by some ghastly common consent, so that by the time his 'Excuse me, excuse me' progress was complete, she was gone and the table empty even of crumbs.

Then he spent the next restless hour looking, seeing her everywhere in the shape of a dozen others, spying her in a distant crowd, whirling past him on the waltzer, moving across the lawns with a group of women, never once seeing him. The crowds moved like sparrows, debating and screaming at each novelty, fluttering on and off dance floors, around the incessant barbecues, the indoor cabaret, the disco, leaving tables empty until exhaustion struck, and whenever he saw her, she was not remotely approachable. He knew it was chance. A kind of weary fatalism overtook him, but still he looked.

Her movements had become frenetic. She had not bargained for being hunted. First there had been the initial embarrassment, probably worse for them she hoped, of encountering so many of the men from her past and present. Men whom she met alone, now firmly attached to other women, the men who had paid for the dress she wore. There they all were, in various combinations, glimpsed or met with partners on arms and Sarah introduced as a new acquaintance. There was Judge Albemarle, eyebrows in sky with a look of discomfited, amused surprise. 'How do you do, Miss Fortune? Have we met before?' 'No, I don't think I have the privilege of Your Honour's acquaintance . . .' Sarah's reply.

'And how do you do, Mrs Albemarle?' facing a grim smile from that lady who was eyeing the drink in her husband's hand with weary and puritan distaste. Then there was Michael the Mole, only recently persuaded towards better things, but still sporting not a wife, but a mother, strange man in his choice of persecutions. Then James, grinning from ear to ear, winking uncontrollably, nervous with laughter but masking it, just. How nice to see you all, how very nice. Yes, the lights and the band, and everything are, is wonderful. I'm very well, thank you. See you next week. We have a conference, I think, said Henry.

Surprising how accurate each description was. She could always picture the partners and there they were. Maybe it was the facility of lawyers to talk so well. By the time she had found herself shaking hands with Leo the Lemon after Hugo Hyperactive, serenity was becoming difficult in the face of the constant threat of a serious fit of giggles, and her only gratitude was for the size of the crowd and the anonymity of it all. Sarah Fortune's entire legal cabal on parade, all in their Sunday best, the one funny aspect which appealed beneath the respectable glitter, the badges of honour, the judges' sashes and the general celebration of sublimely respectable status quo, none of it quite as it seemed, like a picture without focus. And then when she had absorbed the cynicism of this into a sense of its own joke and straightened out her face, ready for the next onslaught on self-control, she had felt, rather than seen, the presence of Charles Tysall, like unseemly fungus on a pair of shoes.

Difficult to fly through a press of people. She was not

running as such, not in an evening dress, although that was the instinct, but merely sliding away gracefully round the edge of the lawns, out through the side gate used by the gardener, into a narrow lane of parked cars, all of them silent and cold even in the close sound of music and crowds. Thumping through the trees, the band began to play a persistent Latin American beat, overtones of flamenco, a kind of tango for those of an age to reminisce, catchy and carefree. Sarah hummed in the darkness, 'Da da da Da' (kick) 'da da da da' (turn) 'da da Da, da da Did ... and then he hid ...' cantered a few exaggerated steps, twirled and turned by herself. Nothing to lose, but I dare not go on that dance floor, Simeon will be worried, and all this is very silly indeed, but I am frightened, and I have always despised my cowardice. The presence of it, the heat of it among the cool shadows of this avenue, made her want to suppress a laughter which was half fear, half scorn.

She walked the length of the cars, calming her mind with observation. Old cars, new cars, small, large, shiny or dirty, looking abandoned. Passing them slowly she wondered which belonged to whom, equating the grandest with the least likely, the worst with the prudent rich, until she saw the battered Volkswagen. Not a memorable car, except for the fact of there being a dog half-way out of the back window, a puppy of a dog with a lolling tongue, announcing delight at the sight of a human face with one quick bark of welcome. The dog had become stuck in the window in a frantic effort to reach her, beginning the effort as soon as she strolled into sight. Sarah laughed in delight, the hunt momentarily forgotten.

'Fine watchdog you are,' she said, stroking the head which pushed itself into her hand. 'Even if you weren't stuck with trying to get out, you'd let anyone steal anything, wouldn't you? There now, what's the matter? No, you can't come out. You wouldn't like it, I promise you, they're all as mad as hatters. Are you thirsty?'

She had noticed an empty enamel dish on the back seat. Dog had been supplied with water, and had finished it in a spate of anxiety. Sarah leaned through the window, opened the door, retrieved the dish, walked back a few steps to the tap at the gardener's gate, replenished the water and returned. She held the dish at chest height while the dog lapped with careless enthusiasm, eyeing her throughout, splashing the purple dress. 'Clumsy,' said Sarah. 'Never mind.' Then she put the empty dish back on the seat, noticing how careful the owner had been to provide comfort in the form of rug and bowl, his only fault being the failure to notice how easily the back window could be pushed by a creature of such agility. 'Can't stay long,' she said cheerfully. 'Only two more hours of hell to go. Now go to sleep. No more trying to get out. You'll be lost. All right?'

She wound the window up further to leave room for air but not for exit, shut the door and left reluctantly. Dog remained silent, remarkably responsive to reassurance, turned on the seat and settled. Sarah braced herself for a return to the fray, wishing that men were more like animals.

Charles had waited and watched, and like cat with mouse, caught her as soon as she emerged into the throng. It was only to be endured with calm. Wherever she turned in

166

whatever company, there he was within yards, smiling his urbane smile, ignoring whatever partner or party, forcing an introduction into Simeon's group which, flushed with its own success, welcomed him with open arms. She could not refuse his choice to avoid the separate twitching of the disco for the closeness of the waltz. 'There, Sarah my dear, was that so painful?' His lazy question into her ear, holding her close with the ease of expertise while she responded to his fluid steps automatically, putting into her feet the irritation, the fear and the beating heart, all stopped in an effort of politeness which overcame distaste. Guiding her away from the floor with a light grip on her arm as effective as a vice, he had led her into the wide gravel of the walks, strolling by force towards the garish lights of the miniature fairground. A pair of romantic walkers, two of many careless, enraptured souls.

'Fancy! There's our Sarah Fortune,' remarked Penelope to her son, as they ambled themselves in the same direction, with Mother unaware of his distraction. Malcolm was silent, his eyes fixed on one graceful, retreating back, struggling with the impulse to run the few steps forward. 'Ernest will be disappointed to have missed her finery,' continued Mama artlessly. 'But just wait till I tell him . . .'

'Tell him what?' asked Malcolm, striving for control. 'Oh no, dear.' She patted his arm. 'Of course you don't know. Well, that girl up there, the one with the red hair? That's Ernest's Sarah, the girl in his office I told you about. And, would you believe it, she's with one of Ernest's oldest clients. Not old himself of course, but he's rich enough to have been a client of Ernest's since he was a boy. Charming man, came to dinner once. Charles Tysall.'

She stopped herself in sudden concern, reminded by the name of Ernest's strange preoccupation. Penelope usually saved words, but now was as good a time as any, and after today, her son would go back to avoiding her bullying again. She pulled him to face her, forcing him to tear his gaze from the scene beyond.

'Malcolm . . . I wouldn't want to spoil the evening for you by saying this, but you must come and see your father. He isn't just worried by the things you said, it's more than that. Seeing Charles Tysall reminded me. It's something to do with Charles, but I don't know what. You know him and his conscience with clients. He keeps their secrets, but wants to burst sometimes. Will you come? Say you will, or I shan't move a step further.'

'Yes,' said Malcolm. 'Of course I shall.' He kept his eyes on Penelope's earnest face, lit yellow from the trees, until her nod allowed him to look back for Sarah. Looking between others, he thought he saw her pull her arm from Charles Tysall's, make a mock curtsey and hurry into the middle of a crowd flanking the paths, darting away in relief. Without the strong arm of a needy mother in his own he could have pursued, but his thoughts, more than his obligations, rooted him to the spot. Charles Tysall, Sarah Fortune, Ernest: all enmeshed somehow, an explosive formula for his ill-prepared mind. He watched the tall man, wondered why Ryan had failed to stress his extraordinary good looks, saw him moving now, unhurriedly but purposefully, in the direction of Sarah's flight, and could not listen to his mother's words, or any words. In his own eyes the glittering, ever-moving crowds of Gray's Inn, the richest and fairest of London's legal society, resembled clown-like children amidst the glowing lights and fairground noises which gave them all the horror of painted and poisoned creatures. Beneath the gaiety, the dignity, the high spirits and the now flushed faces, the lawyers entertained in style such strange corruptions of themselves. He hated them for their stupidity as much as he suddenly despised Sarah Fortune for the nature of the company she deigned to keep. He would never find her in time. On the way down, she had said. More than half-way down to be the glittering consort of a wealthy, dignified thief. Malcolm placed his mama in the gentle care of her friends and made his polite excuses.

At home, the image of her softened. Damn them all for fools, but not Sarah, please not Sarah. Let him find her now he knew how, but he was no longer sure if he should look. He had so small a right to intrude upon a life, whatever he had seen of it, simply because it had intruded so dramatically upon his own. Perhaps he had only needed the search. Malcolm felt entirely powerless.

Dog had greeted him with the usual affection, calmer than he expected, but in his car was a strange, sweetly familiar smell, like a distant memory. There was no pretence in Dog's contentment: to her, the scent was no new experience, nor the height and colours of what she had seen. From the windows of Malcolm's flat, Dog had seen what he had failed to see, the red-haired vision of a former mistress, and had poised

169

herself for adoration. Dog had found her after two long years of distracted searching, and was happy in the discovery.

In the hall of Gray's Inn, amid the Elizabethan splendour festooned with the judges' portraits, the crowd swayed to the alternative band of defiant reggae music. Points Dextrous and his troupe held them in thrall, even the older crowd on the minstrels' gallery, jigging surreptitiously in the dark, while below their faces cigarette smoke caught the floodlights in a haze of brilliant blue like a magician's flare. 'D'ya love me, honey?' yelled the band, 'd'ya love me?' while Charles skirted the crowd in mounting anger, stood on the gallery, the only immobile figure in that vast room, looking for a familiar swathe of colour and a familiar red head. Elisabeth, Porphyria, I shall find you.

Outside, at the back of the hall, servants' entrance for the use of, Sarah sat in the van which had brought Points Dextrous, his crew and all their electronics this evening. She sat on an upturned box, playing cards with Winston the driver, a bottle of wine between them. She had seen the open door, and found the only place to hide.

'Give us a break. Let me sit in here for a bit. Please.'

'What for? What you want, lady? Leave me alone. I'm sleeping.'

'Big man after me.'

'Very big man?'

'Well, very tall.'

Winston had chuckled. 'No surprise, lady. Come in. What you got there?'

'Bottle of wine.'

'Welcome, lady. You play brag?'

'Surely. Not as well as you.'

'We'll see. Close that door. No, not all the way. We needs the light.'

In the same uncertain vehicle, wedged between amplifiers and noisy conversation, Sarah had arrived home without question.

'I owe you a fiver, Winston. As well as a taxi fare.'

'You'll find me, honey. You'll find me. My pleasure. But you're needing more practice when it comes to cards . . .'

Dawn again. Another dawn with the same characteristic effect on flagged spirits. There was damp dew on cool grass, that peculiar and complete silence of the inner city. Pausing on the grass in the joy of being home, she thought what a nice man was Winston, how nice were they all, how lucky to find them. It had always been her only criterion, whatever the rest: they had to be nice, with the description 'nice' used in its least insulting sense. Decent, intelligent, kindly men, otherwise it would never have worked, she would never have got herself on the boil for the whole enterprise. And that brought about the whole vexed problem and the only source of guilt: how to cope when she actually, genuinely liked them all, wanted them to pay, but all the same could never give a bad deal, always wanting the best for each and every one of them. Neither a borrower nor a lender be, and no, she had been neither. Good value Sarah, with high value fellows and plenty of laughter. No reason why not, she had never seen why not. Respectable wives charged higher for services far more basic, not even dignified by the business arrangement it was. Not that she ever justified herself by this, or any other comparison.

Her mind turned to the clients, oddly comforted by them. All found by accident and design, in the very respectable corners of her own profession, discovered in barristers' chambers, court room foyers, meetings, even on the phone, by Temple Lawns and High Court annexes, her daily places and theirs. The more distinguished the face, the more the features could show the pressure, the greater was the need focused there, and sympathy was no less mutual whether or not it carried her own particular price tag. They found her without asking; she was simply there. For a lawyer, a lawyer mistress was a godsend, so discreet. A peculiar bonus if she made you laugh, so genuinely good at listening to worries. As far as she knew, she trampled on no one else's territory. This was not theft, it was simply an abundance of need and a dearth of companionship, paid for in familiar coin, dignified by affection.

Kicking the grass, smelling the air, she wondered if they all knew their nicknames. Probably. She had never hidden them, never hidden anything, except for all the things they quite deliberately failed to ask, such as, are there others apart from me? Better not to know, although they must silently have guessed. None of them were stupid; she could never have stood a stupid man. Even Hurried Hugo, workaholic with the ever-absent wife. Simeon, of course, known as Smoke, anxious widower. Georgie Albemarle, known as the dawn-raider for calling at six a.m., completing the inevitable within minutes,

172

talking for an hour and a half (What sentence would you give this one, Sarah? Oh, as little as possible, I think. Be kind today. Good, I'm glad you agree . . .), all before departing with the wig and gown left by the door. It was the talking which seemed to matter most with all of them, the listening rather, and she never knew for what comfort they paid, had certainly never thought of sex and law as any kind of erotic combination. Which it was, even to James, Tax barrister, known fondly as Ticker because of a bad heart and the habit of counting in his sleep, and Henry Hypochondria, who knew hugging was good for his health. So far, she was committed to two mornings, two lunchtimes and three evenings a week. Her bank balance was healthy, there was the beginning of an escape route from the hatred of work, and even if her sense of humour and her energy was under strain, life was still tenable. As long as they were what they were, kindly, normal, needy men, quite rightly greeted with affection, lost with calm regret, and frequently as the result of her own advice. Go, young old man, don't bother paying me, I enjoyed you. You have better things to conquer, now you know how. She was not good at collecting fees, tended to forget them. Fun and money, never mind law, sex and secrecy, all made for different, attractive combinations, suitable for an outsider who had ceased to care.

'I'm a tart,' she told the moon. 'Tart with heart. And that means I have to get Winston to drive me home. I'm so rich with uncollected fees I come home by van. Think I can take it?'

What the hell. She threw the evening bag in the air, caught it and ran indoors.

CHAPTER ELEVEN

The summer was glorious, but it had been a long hard year, almost beyond curing. Ryan felt the lassitude of the heat, dogged by the slower pace of life he had come to adopt so easily on his country holiday, felt his brain was dulled, leaving only enthusiasm without energy, questions without answers. Besides, he had fallen in love with his own wife, embarrassing to say the least, dulling all memories, all other instincts. On his return he did not seek out Malcolm Cook with his slender store of fresh knowledge which all looked so insignificant against the grime of London, only spoke on the phone, sat in his stuffy office, his back to the small view of the sky, thinking of the sun and his wife in her blue bikini. Bailey had found him there.

'You look well. How was it?'

'Bloody marvellous. Great to be back. What's the news?'

The irony of the tone, accompanied by the rueful grin, made Bailey pleased to see him.

'I see a man with contentment oozing out of every pore,

174

and what do you mean, news? It's all in your in-tray, the alarming size of which I have come to discuss. Any developments on Tysall? Either before you left, or since? You'll notice I was patient enough not to ask sooner.'

'Nope. Nothing doing, then or now. I found out that the Tysall wife threw away her credit cards in Norfolk. I think she's probably dead up there.'

'And that's all?'

'Yes.'

'Nothing else, in three months?'

'No. Nothing. Gone to ground. He plays at home and keeps his nose clean. No rumours, no reports, nothing.'

Bailey sat down, heavy with disappointment. 'Nothing. Only a civil action against the Commissioner listed for hearing in the autumn. Expensive claims for loss of profit and harassment. Perhaps that's why he's quiet. Certainly a reason, so I'm warned, why we should be the same. Anyway, enough's enough. Until we can say someone's in danger, we have to call it a day. Even unofficially.'

Ryan thought of his garden with sudden longing, irritated to miss the tranquillity of knowing where his wife was and what she was doing.

'Yes, I suppose we do. Stop, I mean. Funny, I don't really mind. Maybe I'll mind when the weather's cooler. For now, and for once, I want a quiet life.'

A depressed mood, Bailey sensed, the somnolence of enforced leisure. Then Bailey remembered Ryan had kept an eye on Tysall for two years, a long time for a man with a preference for quick results.

'Have you spoken to Malcolm Cook? I know he was interested.'

'Well, yes, a phone call. Nice bloke, Malcolm. We were going to have a drink, but he couldn't this week. I get the impression he's fed up hearing me bellyaching about Tysall. No one wanted to know apart from me.' There was a note of mournful self-pity, provoking Bailey to brisk reply.

'Best leave it then. For now.'

'All right, sir.' There was the familiar wolfish grin. 'For now.'

'He'll come back, Ryan. They always do.'

'I know, sir, I know.'

Ryan might be growing up at last. 'Never flog a dead horse, or you'll never make old bones yourself. Let sleeping dogs lie. My new philosophy, or should be. If you see what I mean.'

'I do,' said Bailey, mouth twitching at the mixture of metaphors. 'But I thought you'd mind.'

'So did I,' answered Ryan. 'But just at the moment, I don't. Much.'

Malcolm's indifference to Ryan's cheerful voice so soon after the discoveries of Gray's Inn Lawns was not entirely calculated, nor had he meant it to sound as clear as it had. It was simply the fact that he did not know what to do, and had no wish to discuss Charles Tysall until he was able to discover the role of the man in the life of one Sarah Fortune. He had no doubt that his father could assist with his knowledge of one or the other, but it was all a question of how to ask. Now he actually knew where she was, he was reluctant

176

to act on the knowledge without acquiring more, afraid of treading on toes. So he waited. With all his lawyer's caution, Malcolm had never really believed in Ryan's ogre, and the belief was lessened by the awareness of the innate respectability of his stepfather's clientele. He did not consider that their respectability was anything more than surface, but could not envisage his father allowing thief and psychopath through the portals. Such characters, a source of fascination to himself, would bring nothing but revulsion for Ernest. Now, having seen Charles in company with Sarah, he hoped that his own assumptions were true, and willed them to be so. He was neither wilfully optimistic nor careless, but on the day when he would have pursued his father, healed the rift and found his answers, Ernest Matthewson was proving elusive. Until he could find his father, Malcolm did not wish to speak to Ryan, but the more he tried to make contact, the more he met with frustration. Ernest had chosen this day to disappear.

When Malcolm telephoned, Ernest was first of all sitting in a dim West End pub, then, on the second occasion, sitting in another, both chosen deliberately for their down-at-heel anonymity. Ernest was on a bender. An anniversary, that is what it was. A remembrance of the same day two years before, when Mrs Elisabeth Tysall had telephoned from a Norfolk call-box and asked him to help. 'Please, Ernest, please . . . I know you belong to Charles, but please . . . ' He remembered how the word 'belong' had stung him, as if he needed a reminder even then. It had made him stiff with resentment, so that he had said, in his most pompous tones,

'I don't actually belong to either of you, but if I did, it would have to be to your husband, Elisabeth. He pays for exclusive service, so I don't know if I could help you.' As the phone had been gently and hopelessly replaced, he had regretted the words, and in the light of all he had learned since, regretted them more.

Hiding from the office, hiding from home, with an ache in his side and a bad conscience, all compounded by the nagging anxiety inspired by Pen's careless account of the Ball, and who she had seen with whom. Time for Ernest to break the habits of a lifetime, swallow his pride and enlist the advice of his stepson. Plodding further and further away from his office he could feel the pain which heralded sickness, worried by the prospect of a familiar pattern of stress and the prospect of seeing the son he had failed to meet for so long.

Deal with the stress first, his doctor had said. Do nothing else today, except hide, and make a resolution for tomorrow. Today was an ill-starred day. Leave it until tomorrow. Today he would think it out; tomorrow he would speak. And after that, he might salve his conscience if possible, take Pen down to the coastline which had been the scene of that haunting phone call from the woman he hoped still lived, who had been the source of his misery since. He was comforted by the thought of a journey of retribution. Wherever it was, this place from which she had spoken, he had always imagined it calm, blue and somehow sublimely peaceful.

*

178

The wind had blown, loud and chill, up the channels the week before, driving the tide to a new fury, so that even the boy was afraid, turning back to look for drier land before the water moved. Before this, he had stayed out until the last minute, pitting himself against the tide's speed, playing games with it, calculating close odds on which of them would win his self-appointed challenge, risking all the time. Now he did not dare: the weather was dangerous, the water unpredictable, making him turn and run before it, quickened with fear. The fishermen laughed at his anxiety: now you'll learn, boy, nothing stays the same, didn't you realise? You think you know these channels like the back of your hand, but they break in these freak tides, split and crumble in the floods, never quite the same again. Find a new place for your boat. Last time this happened the sea came closer and killed your father. Don't be surprised.

In the summer storms none feared the results more than the new stepfather, but inevitably, it was the boy himself who found her in the same spot where those exhausting attempts had been made to spare his eyes. Sand-woman, stained brown, clothed, but not recognisably so, imperfectly preserved in sand, mud and salt, scarcely human. She was betrayed by the existence of limbs and hair, the bones of five toes and fingers, but difficult to imagine she had ever breathed, or put the clothes on that decayed body, let alone spoken words through the sand-filled orifice which had once been a mouth. Slack tide when he found her, as indifferent as that mouth; part of the bank crumbled away, split itself into a fissure six feet deep, with fragments of mud left for the next

179

tide's shifting, and there she was, a brown, lumpish thing lying in the gap, only the head of her washed into something vaguely recognisable, a shiny forehead, free of flesh. The boy had looked closely, then he was sick, and half ran, half waded to the safety of the quay.

No time to reach the pathologist before the tide swept back. Dear God, what was the point, she was very dead already. He could wait, so that after the boy had found his uncle and a posse of men he could lead them back. They believed him and followed willingly, but having looked and retched, all they could do was carry her back in the boat before the water caught her again. Her skull was covered, her mud-heavy skirt pulled down decently.

Ah, poor creature. A death not like a violent city death, made worse by this involuntary and undignified disinterment. Poor, poor creature, the doctor said. He was never a stranger to tears.

Take this down, I cannot write and examine at the same time. Colour of hair, red. (They had washed a morsel of it; even below the sand it had grown into a wild mane.) Human type: Caucasian. Eyeless, sand-stained, no colour left on the hefty brown remnants of flesh even after hosing down, but cleft to the cheekbones, skin might have shown scars. Hands: long, clever, some broken fingers, either cut or crushed, the skin receded from them. A slim-built, proportional woman of thirty summers, possibly more. Most likely cause of death under the sea, water in the lungs, in common parlance, drowning. Extracts from the bone marrow revealing the presence of the same diatoms found in the surrounding sea, proof she had died in these waters and not in any others. Impossible to say what had been in that bloodstream apart from salt, and equally hard to be certain about the times. No telltale organisms beneath the sand, the pathologist explained, not like a body in a field where he could have collected the squirming life still breeding on the carrion and sent them away for someone else to judge the time of death by the dreadful cycle of the predators. A dipocere, a waxy lard, present in abundance, preserving shape. She had been buried deep, most likely within a few hours of death to remain as recognisable as this. Before she began to hum, someone joked grimly. Clothes, synthetic material, virtually intact. Some damage by marine life. The eyes long since gone, the toes no more than bone. Another decomposition expert said again, poor creature, reckoned at least a year, never more than eighteen months since she had first lain there. All discussed in the pub on the quay, with the stepfather breathing a sigh of relief, thinking how well it was for experts to be so certain. Police Constable Curl looked at his brother and his nephew, shrewdly remained silent, as did they, the boy as taciturn as usual. Having each other, the mother and the sea, they needed neither trouble nor questions. They did not even form a conspiracy. As a silence, it was simply complete.

But Constable Curl remembered Ryan, and remembered what little else he knew on the science of dead bodies. Someone would find out who she was because of the teeth, even less destructible than those plastic cards. Dentists, strange beings, would be sent a diagram of those less than perfect, if only slightly mended, teeth and one of them would recognise that picture as easily as others would recognise a face. Experts in death found people by teeth even if there was nothing else left, and it only took days. Hardly the concern of PC Curl, but after many hours, with the London copper in his slow mind, the Norfolk constable telephoned Detective Sergeant Ryan. No point him saying it then, but he had known as soon as he lifted the decomposed legs of her into the boat, exactly who she was. What he could not fathom was who it was who had buried her.

Maria was submerged beneath blankets in her own tiny room when Ted had found her. Thin thing, lithe as a lizard, dark honey-coloured hooker, kind-hearted kid. As he looked at her swollen eyes and reddened cheeks, he could see in the pulsing finger marks on her shoulders the souvenirs of larger hands grasping smaller bones. In the distant memory of a luckier youth before he discovered the experience of constant abuse, Ted pitied Maria, weeping not for a lost life, but with all the confusion of a wounded animal.

'What's up?' He knelt by the side of her unmade bed, and smelt Tysall. 'Here, you silly girl, show me what he did.'

Slapped, that was all, held by one hand, slapped by the other, with fingers on that tiny throat. He could feel them, almost see them. Two bloodshot eyes, no white spots of suffocation, not so bad, although her ears must still be ringing. 'Bastard,' he muttered, 'bastard.' She winced slightly at the touch of his hands.

'He pull my hair, Ted. Says nothing, suddenly goes bang,

Teddie. What did I do? Don't know why. He pull my hair very hard.'

'Who pulled your hair?' As if he did not know. She sighed.

'Who you think, Teddie? Mr Charles, who else? Bad man.'

'First time?'

'First time, yes, but before I was very careful. I leave too quick for him to do what he wants, then go, whoosh! In, out, run away. But I knew he would, one day; I always knew he would. That kind, Charlie boy. Not so bad, Ted, I promise; not so bad. I stop crying now. You buy me drink.'

'You can have a bucketful, sweetheart. Go and bathe those eyes.' Her thin arms clung around his neck, then she dried her eyes carefully. Ted could only stand so much of that; he would go if she kept on crying. He held her briefly, suddenly bereft, wondering if the state of her face were some kind of revenge.

It had been a Machiavellian touch in Charles to link the two of them in his service, worse to have seen them both in the same afternoon. They had been in Tysall's flat within hours of each other, separate times and entirely separate purposes; he at noon, Maria at four. Perhaps Maria had paid for the understated insolence which Ted had been unable to control; the thought made him clench his fists in impotent rage, relax at the thought of his own helplessness. He should not have taken a drink before arriving to make the report of the last two months' work, resenting his captivity in those graceful rooms as soon as he walked through the door, knowing that every word he repeated of his illegal activities put him further into Tysall's hands, further beyond pale normality, and deeper into the realms of blackmail. Being so thoroughly in Tysall's power had made him enjoy the man's discomfiture, but it seemed now as if Maria had paid. Ted did not count who else.

The profile on the life and times of one Sarah Fortune had been episodic, compiled over twelve weeks as far as Tysall's expense account was concerned, although Ted had discovered all he needed to know in less time than that, with a little help. Yes, he answered diffidently, he had been to the home today, and here were the keys Mr Tysall had obtained himself and Ted had used, safe on the table, while in his head was a history of her daily rituals. All of them, nothing excluded, from the early morning visitors to the destinations of her taxi rides, and the occasional, oddly misspent lunch hour. Ted knew whom she saw and the purpose of the meetings, and did not omit his own firm conclusions as to what this beautiful woman did in all her respectability, with any time about her slender person which could be called spare. However, he did not say why she did it, since even he could not account for that. Nor why this peculiar lack of vulgarity or greed in her, as well as a dearth of any conspicuous riches in her clothes, her choice of shops, her acquaintances.

'Do you really expect me to believe this?'

'I'm not paid to lie. Sir. Nor would I bother recording it if it wasn't what I'd seen. And concluded. Sir.'

Soberly said. Ted felt he could afford this hint of sneering in the face of the white shock on Charles Tysall's face. That shade of insolence in Ted's voice was registered, but provoked no instant retribution. Charles walked to the window, spoke softly.

'The woman's a whore.'

Ted shrugged, waiting in the silence. What was the point in telling Tysall, yes she was, but she was so much more than that; someone he had actually grown to like through simply observing her? A woman who took out stray kids on Sundays and had them screeching with joy; whose paying men regarded her with genuine affection? Not for him to describe how she was patient and popular, loved or liked by all who dealt with her. And what the hell was wrong with being a tart in the first place, keeping other men's desires as well as their secrets, and in this case, as far as he could see, preserving their sanity as well. It was not inconsistent in Ted's mind that a female of these proclivities should be also a funny and generous woman. Considerate, kindly Sarah Fortune proved it was possible, but the word 'whore' had been pronounced like a whispered curse.

'I didn't say that, with respect.' Ted's vocabulary still borrowed from the judicial. 'I was simply suggesting that, discreetly as may be, she sees plenty of men.'

'And keeps accounts of them, no doubt.'

'Possibly. Probably. Well, yes.'

Charles stood by his wide window, his back to Ted, while Ted stood uncomfortably in the middle of the floor, hands crossed behind back, shifting his weight occasionally and imperceptibly as he had learned through hours of waiting. He preferred to stand. Sitting rendered the relationship even more unequal, and standing he allowed himself a fleeting smile in the mirror.

'Damn Porphyria,' said Charles loudly, but absently. 'She was supposed to be perfectly pure and good.'

'What did you say, sir?'

The insolence was becoming more pronounced. Ted clenched his teeth to restrain it.

'Did you know,' said Charles, spinning on his heel and striding towards Ted so swiftly that he had brought them face to face before the words were fully formed, 'that my wife was a whore? And I have been combing the ranks of women to find her equal, as perfect in all respects, but without that fatal flaw. Did you know that?'

The words emerged with such venom that Ted stepped back, drew in his chest to increase the distance between them.

'But she wasn't . . . ' No, she had not been anything of the kind as Ted recalled, a little flighty maybe, but not his concern until the end.

'It's not my business to know anything of the kind, sir.'

'Good.'

Charles wandered back to the window. Ted was shaken, wondered if he was dismissed.

'Won't have me, the bitch? She'll learn,' said Charles so quietly the words were no more than an outward breath.

'How, sir?'

Ted had finally spoken out of turn; he closed his mouth abruptly.

'That's all. Get out. Leave me the keys and get out. Forget all this, will you? My regards to young Maria.' The last words were affably accompanied by a smile. Ted had wanted to slap him. Instead, he left without gesture or word.

Looking now at Maria's face, Ted was glad his report had been incomplete; more pleased still that he had not mentioned to Tysall the nuisance factors and all the coincidences which had made his task so bizarre. First, the connection with Joan which had helped so much; then, that bloody dog loping across the park last night, following the jogger into the nether regions of Sarah Fortune's house. Elisabeth Tysall's dog, then Ted's own dog; the impotence of seeing that animal was the last factor which made him try to warn her. A light warning, only by moving the chair a fraction, putting his fingers on the mirror which dominated the hall. He would have liked her less had her rooms been pristine, without the postcards showing normality, the dust on the mirror, the creased clothes. But in all of her belongings, there had been this strange and total absence of any vanity, and under its spell, against all his instincts, he had left some trace of himself and touched the mirror, moved the chair in one room, and hoped for her observation.

A woman so different from Maria. No powers of observation here beyond the minimum necessary for a creature of instinct, not a calculating mind like his own, currently moving with speed. Maybe Tysall would do nothing more; far more predictable that he should simply watch, but even if he merely abandoned his pursuit for less direct retribution, it was time for Ted to move on. With this skinny little outsider, perhaps; not ever with Joan and his children. Somehow the sight of the dog he had brought to them, so carelessly stolen from himself, underlined for him how far he had gone from ever being forgiven for what he was, or from making decisions at all. He had better try to save something from this. He put an arm round Maria's shoulder, and with the other hand reached for the whisky she had left for him on the table.

CHAPTER TWELVE

Propped up against the desk was the bouquet. Two dozen roses, twelve carnations in a savage harmony of red, offset with a cloud of fern and a crimson ribbon, like a funeral tribute. One tasteful card. *CT.*

'Joan!'

'Yes?' No longer hovering for Sarah's arrival, Joan's startling look of guilt was almost as disturbing as the relentless colour of the flowers themselves. She had waited for Sarah's presence, nerving herself: today I shall say something. I shall tell her about Ted and all the rest, see what she thinks. I must tell her. About love's not-so-young dreamer. No harm in it, of course, but I must tell her. She's never been bad to me, I have to admit that. I should say something; she's never done me wrong, not in years. After she's seen the flowers; she'll surely like the flowers. Then I'll say something, but I'm not sure what.

'Who brought these?'

'Oh, a messenger, I suppose. All right for some.'

'I would like to know,' said Sarah quietly, 'how a messenger would know that I would be here to receive them. No one sends flowers into a vacuum.'

'I told him.'

'Told who?'

'Charles Tysall. Does it matter?'

The hurt and bewilderment in Sarah's flushed face, the sudden understanding of some kind of subtle betrayal, made Joan wince.

'Does it matter, Sarah? Don't be so silly. They're only bloody flowers.'

'Joan, I asked you weeks ago, don't answer Charles Tysall, and if he rings, tell him I'm out. Why didn't you do as I asked?'

Joan was silent, struggling for words, mulish in her confusion. Then shrugged her shoulders, the worst and least attractive in her repertoire of self-defensive gestures, angry for feeling bad. Sarah's sense of isolation grew. She looked at the flowers, smelt the suffocating scent of blooms in warm cellophane, felt the tears of disappointment at the back of her eyes, and straightened her spine.

'All right. If you say so, Joan, of course it doesn't matter, but I thought you might know I wouldn't avoid anyone without good reason. Never mind. Not important. I'd better do some work.'

She softened the dismissal with a bright smile, but in Joan's condition it was the dismissal alone which registered.

With the high colour and step of a puppet soldier she left the room of flowers and shut the door on her own sanctum with a crash. No telling secrets now which would have burst forth a few minutes ago. She might have wanted to confess, but forced herself into a kind of irritation instead, made conspicuous noises of industry, banging cabinet-drawers, typing with loud and furious inaccuracy. Let . . . it . . . bloody wait. She was there to work, shop, go home. Let . . . it . . . wait until Madam was more receptive. Joan made anger the companion to conscience.

Home early on the train, swaying with the flowers pressed against the back of the crowd, thinking fast and slow. I feel what I am, odd, outcast and cast out. Living in a way removed from anyone else, with no feelings much. Except fear, for the first time, fear. Waiting for the ghost of the following footsteps which had seemed to trail her days. Carnations and roses. Reminiscent of the last funeral, one husband buried at his own request on a hill, with all those wreaths, dead or dying, what was the difference? I loved you. There was nothing left for me but my own kind of promiscuous sympathy after that. Anything for fun, freedom, admiration and the promise of self-sufficiency. Until now. I am alive again now because I am afraid. You were worth it, you know, whatever you did, and I know it now for the first time. I might even do the same again, love someone like that.

She flung the bouquet into the skip at the edge of the small park near the flat, watched the weight of the monster thing drag itself from the top, turned and saw the last flash of crimson as she ran up the steps to the front door, sorry for

191

the blooms. Then inside. Someone had been there. Almost imperceptible traces, all reflected in the large mirror at the end of the hall. Only a chair moved, a smear on the carpet and on the dust, nothing at all. Gremlins, walking around in the emptiness, nothing. Something to make her back away, promise herself to return later, when the gremlins had gone to join the flowers.

'We are looking for Mr Charles Tysall, sir. Wondered if you might have his current address on your files.'

'Of course,' said Ernest stupidly, caught in the emptiness of his office at seven in the evening, more than slightly drunk, bereft of secretary, clueless. 'Who are you?'

'North Norfolk Constabulary, sir.'

'But why,' asked Ernest, looking with slow despair at the bank of slung files in the girl's room, 'do you want to find my client? And why don't you know where he lives? Sorry, too many questions. But I should ask, you know. Protocol. Must protect my client's interests.' He hiccoughed.

'Of course, sir. We do know, actually. But we found your address in his office, and no one seems to know where he is. Or won't say. Same difference isn't it?' The disembodied voice managed a polite laugh, and Ernest tittered in response.

'Hope the bastard's in trouble.'

'What did you say, sir?' The voice had sharpened. Ernest dragged himself upright in his large office chair, remembered his duties to his customer. Father would be ashamed of him now, drunk during office hours for the first time in years, with a gnawing pain in his guts. No pleasure without pain – he should have known better.

192

'Nothing at all . . . officer. But I have to know why you need to know. If you see what I mean.'

There was a pause. 'Well, sir, we think we've found his wife, and we need to contact him. As a matter of urgency.'

'Oh.' Ernest squinted at the ceiling, remembered her voice with a sudden surge of pleasure. 'Oh. I'm glad. Is she asking for him?'

'No, sir, as it happens.' The voice could not resist its own sense of irony. 'If we're right, she's been dead for some considerable time. Eighteen months, we're told. I'd say about two years. Can you hear me, sir?'

Ernest slumped to the floor, holding the receiver away from the strange buzzing in his ears. The voice went on, more urgent, fainter all the time. Sliding into unconsciousness, slipping to the floor, Ernest hoped that the place of this death had been the same as the blue and tranquil scene he had imagined.

By midnight, Malcolm ceased the effort to find either parent and let himself out of the flat for the comfort of darkness. After a slow, sluggish, long run, returning fit enough for sleep but not inclined to it, troubled still, restless for the light which would excuse wakefulness. Only Dog was tired, recovering in sight of home.

He felt a pang of conscience. Dog was not so strong that he should encourage her to run so far. Rest, girl, where are you? Snuffling in the rubbish by the side of the skip at the entrance to their small piece of grass. Wrong again, he told himself. She still has plenty of energy, more than you, in those spindly legs of hers, half her body weight recovered in these few weeks of companionship. 'Dog? Where are you?' Standing in the middle of the green, he shouted for her rather than whistled in front of the big silent houses which stood around them in a large, solid crescent, dim windows, scarce street lamps. Shouting never disturbed such heavy doors, and Malcolm hated to whistle for a dog. A dog was like a child; you did not whistle for a child. Back she rolled, obedient by instinct, bearing her gift.

With all her impulses for kissing, Dog also had the tendencies of a kleptomaniac, and now she was holding in her muzzle her favourite substance, the cellophane rustling and crinkling after her, a red ribbon trailing from her teeth and several battered flowers held in her mouth with difficulty. Malcolm bent to see, curious about her treasures. She shied away, hoping for a game, mock-snarling, scampering off. Play with me, please, play with me, pretty please. Look what I've found. Slowly he followed her back across the kicked-up grass, noticing more of the flowers, carnations scattered in the dog's path, and by the skip, the remnants of the large bouquet, dispersed by nose and paws as she had parted the elaborate wrappings, wanting nothing but the sound of the cellophane.

'Give it to me, girl. Time to go home ...' She barked, quick protest and sudden urgency. Downwind with the flowers, she had caught the new scent, familiar and friendly. Shying away again, she scampered to the big front door, snapping, inviting him to follow. 'Silly girl, why? You know we go in the side, like we always do ... Come back.' But Dog pushed at the door with a wet nose, dropped the cellophane, waited. Puzzled and amused, Malcolm went up the steps in turn, used the unfamiliar key on his key-ring to humour her, opened the door. Even as the handle turned inwards, Dog sped before him, leaving him whispering empty commands. Here, girl, here, highly conscious of being a trespasser in the unfamiliar regions of his own house, following her in sheer exasperation. He paused mid-step, arrested by muffled sounds above his head.

London was huge and endless, full, she had once been told, of golden opportunity, and in the middle of it Sarah had walked, careless of the danger zones. Watched lights from hills and buildings, hopes reflected in the river from Blackfriars Bridge. Place of glorious chance and exciting dwellings, all of them barred to the homeless. She walked endlessly, to court danger and destroy the fear which had driven her out of her own abode; walked to find amusement in whatever she saw and calm the imagination which made her so restless, anything to restore the humorous equilibrium by which she lived. But there was a limit to walking. Her steps formed a circumference around known places and familiar sights, leading her away from strange territory, while all the time she knew she was moving because staying still would show her how much she wanted to talk, and there was no one to listen. She concluded this without self-pity; a fact of life was all it was. No family who would respond, no man whose home territory was sanctuary, her own way. Outsiders live on the outside, without any avenues inwards; she must live with that as she had always done. Slowly but surely, the combination of darkness and light soothed her, and by one o'clock, she had reached the big front door of her own building, solidly silent, with the park beyond bathed in moonlight. Walking for miles had been a meaningless gesture: she had known in the end there was nowhere else to go.

Unlocking the door, Sarah regretted her own anonymity, her total ignorance of all who lived alongside her. The block was almost empty; two occupants on the top floor she guessed, strangers both, one either end, with a tranquillised couple dead to the world on the side ground floor, and herself on the second-floor centre, no more than a fleeting glimpse, a polite curiosity seen at the end of a busy day. All the rest of the small family, successful couples who lived in this semi-elegance, had sloped away earlier on the same day, last Friday of school holidays, leaving behind no trace of childish weeping and wailing to mix with the hum of the city silence. Slower still, she climbed the stairs. Don't be silly, your imagination has stolen your sanity. You are not important enough for anyone to watch you. Get indoors, have a glass of wine and go, to sleep. Besides you have no choice. What else do you do, knock on the door of some stranger neighbour and say, come inside my own flat with me please? Provocative thought which made her smile. She could always wait outside for the jogger, who latterly had shown no sign of life, equally out of the question, and besides, it was only a question of opening the door. She unlocked it with quiet confidence and a sigh of relief. Cured of anxiety all by herself, proud of it.

Half-subdued instinct warned her immediately of some other presence, and she dispelled the thought, pausing on the threshold and waiting for the sound of breath, hearing none. Then flinging down her bag, feeling foolish for a wasted evening, walking boldly up the short passage to run a bath, without closing the door behind her, whistling as she went, happy to be back. Stopped suddenly as she saw the mirror at the end, catching the reflections of the rooms on either side, silent tribute to good taste, giving an immediate view of all her possessions, but always dusty.

There was no movement, no sound from him, only a profile of his face behind the mirror. A composed face, immobile like his stance, as if he had ceased to breathe. He was not hiding, simply waiting in one room, their eyes caught in the glass obliquely before she could turn back towards the door. The statue of him sprang into life as soon as the whistling died on her tongue. Charles's reaction was instantaneous, peculiar facility for a man so languid and controlled. He was behind her, grabbing the thick hair in the same moment she had turned to run.

'Don't scream,' he said. 'There's no point screaming and I detest women screaming.'

Sarah stood still and did not scream. She clenched her hands by her side to stop the trembling, mastered it slowly while he waited, holding her so close she could feel the buckle of his belt pressed into the small of her back, close as any lover, but holding in his hands two fistfuls of hair.

'Sarah,' he said. 'Porphyria. Perfectly pure and good, I thought. Now I know better.'

She did not speak. There was the impediment of terror as well as the knowledge of futility. A stranger in possession of a key to her home, where he had waited, how long she could not guess, was not, she sensed, amenable to even tones, nor would he respond to either questions or orders. So she remained as she was, felt him lift the mane of her hair, and kiss the side of her neck with deliberate coldness. She flinched. The trembling, scarcely controlled, began again.

'Ah, Miss Fortune, afraid? Of me? How could you be? I was ready to give you the world, but you have humiliated me in return. You do not, I hear, flinch in the arms of other men. You sleep in their beds, and they in yours.'

'If I do, that is no concern of yours,' she answered, her voice surprisingly calm.

'Ah, but it is, Porphyria, it is. I wanted you, and all you can do is throw away my flowers, and open your legs for other men.'

She was silenced by the crudeness, thoughts in racing panic. All those footsteps in her mind, the presence of the follower she had never seen, or told herself she had never seen. There emerged some form to the fears she had tried, successfully, to dismiss; they had substance now, but no sense except for the logic of obsession. She tried to apply her mind to that logic and attempted to speak.

'Charles, this is the height of stupidity. Whatever you may need, you have no right to break into my house. Get out, please, before you're discovered. You may be powerful, but you aren't immune.'

He pulled the hair, her neck stretched back in one agonising movement. With her throat pulled taut, she was forced to stare up into the face bent over hers while he laughed briefly at the expression of pain and fear.

'Leave? Before discovery? One of your legal terms, is it not? Who fears discovery? Like a title for a play. You are the one who should have feared that. Besides, why should I have less licence with your house and your body than you give to anyone, everyone else, comparative stranger though I am? I hoped it would be otherwise. And if I leave go of your hair, darling Sarah, what will you do?'

'Call the police,' she hissed, her neck stretched further.

'And have them arrive? Surely not. Granted the benefit of a few details of your life, I doubt they'll see fit to assist you much. They are busier with other battles.'

He paused, allowed the words to sink in, then slowly released her.

They stood facing each other in the hall, the mirror at the end reflecting a picture of part of her own white face in the single light, half-hidden by the lithe, black-clad figure of Charles Tysall. Odd thoughts filtered by panic and puzzlement, such as what a handsome man he was, even now, what a graceful head, what power there was in his slenderness. Should she shudder at the repellent attraction of him, smile, submit, joke, scream, stay silent? The world was asleep in a sleepy building. A policy in these respectable houses to ignore screams. A similar policy for the police, should she be allowed to call them, to do their utmost to protect the innocent, and Sarah knew she would never be one of those.

Not guilty, but not innocent either. The knowledge weakened her, made her weary, beyond questions, reproach or anything other than temporary submission. For anyone weaker or anything requiring protection, for a child, for a friend, a lover, even a dumb animal, she might have fought like a savage, taken him by surprise. For herself, since it had been so long since she had cared for herself at all, even for the protection of her own body, she could not.

'Do what you want, Charles. Whatever you want. Just get it over with.'

'Like any other lover?'

He held her shoulders, turned her, stood back and regarded her face with a quizzical smile.

'Like any other lover,' she said gently, 'if that is what you need.'

Charles sighed exaggerated sadness. 'Ah, Porphyria. You will not even fight. But I forgot. You have no virtue left to protect, have you?'

'More than you think. I do not torment or abuse. I leave when I am not welcome. I am there when I am needed. I do not trespass or take anything from anyone. There is no malice in me. I like to live, that is all. I call that a kind of virtue. More than yours.'

'There are different virtues, then. I do not count those.'

He was stroking her now, his hands cupping her breasts, soft and firm beneath the cotton blouse. In the silence of the house, nothing stirred. She was aware of the open door behind her, equally aware that he had seen it and knew he could afford to ignore whatever remote help may have lain beyond.

'Take off your clothes, Miss Fortune. I have seen other whores. Let us see how you resemble one another.'

She could not see what it was he wanted; rape, or seduction at the knife-point of his presence, or more simply humiliation. Without direction, she hesitated.

'Go on, Miss Fortune. A familiar enough ritual, surely.'

The defensive power, poor though it had been, was gone. So was the power to form any words at all. How to say, yes, undressing was a familiar enough ritual, but not for this, not like this. Whatever I have done, with whoever it was, for money or for love, for simple pleasure or for a gamble, was done to please with at least an element of affection. Not like this. I am an entirely honest animal in my way; I have never cheated. Please do not make me do this. I am ashamed of everything beneath the shell of clothes – who could be otherwise in the presence of one whose sole purpose was to steal everything, perhaps even life, but certainly dignity first? I have always kept that, she thought wildly. I have always kept a little dignity and made sure others did the same. They could always have mine in return for their own. I am not as bad as he suspects, but he would not understand. I had better do as he says, and he may, just may, leave me alone. She undid the buttons on her blouse.

He sat in the chair pulled from the living room, next to the mirror, fingering the stone head on the table next to it, smiling, tapping his fingers.

'Go on,' he said.

She snapped in fury. 'What do you want me to do? Would you prefer I did this to music, like a cabaret act? There are far better ones in the West End.'

Insolent bravado. She watched the jaw tighten and the grimace of a smile faded.

'No, just undress. As I told you. And,' he added, 'watch yourself, here, as you undress.' He moved sideways slightly, so that she could see herself in the mirror. For the first time, she turned her eyes to him in a plea.

'Please . . . I can't do that.'

'You can. You shall. Watch yourself in the glass. And I shall watch you watching.'

She began to cry, a motionless sobbing. Sarah loathed the mirror, hated for years the reflection of that unproductive flesh, whatever the pleasures it had given and received. Conventional clothes, a conventional house, a daytime conventional life, dropping to the floor. First the blouse, revealing tanned shoulders, then the skirt, then the slip. Left in bra and knickers, she hesitated again, saw his face and went on. Unhooked the flimsy piece of cotton last, felt her bosom fall free. Stood upright, resisting an impulse to fold her arms across her chest in memory of that last remnant of pride. She had not always hated this almost-perfect body, but despised it now. Impossible to look into the mirror. She turned her head aside, and waited, the slow trickle of enormous tears on her face the only movement of soundless desperation.

Charles stood up and approached her, twisted her face roughly towards his own, and kissed her mouth. Then moved to stand beside her, so that she was forced to face the mirror while, slowly, he ran his hands down the sides of her body, across the flat stomach, brushed his palms against

202

her nipples. He stroked the cleft of her buttocks, and, bending, touched the bush of her pubic hair. She was shivering uncontrollably.

'I was right,' he said. 'I knew you would be like this, perfect, but perfectly flawed. Look at yourself, what do you see?' He continued to stroke the captive body, and she did not answer. Nakedness made her completely vulnerable, but her silence angered him. When she finally spoke, the repetitious weariness of her answer angered him more.

'Whatever you want, Charles. Just finish whatever you came to do. Whatever you want.'

The body behind her own stiffened, the hands ceased their rhythmic stroke, and placed themselves, disembodied, in the mirror, around her neck.

'Do you think it is as simple as that? I wanted you to want me, but how could any man want you now? Put myself inside you, diseased as you are . . . I am so tired of women like you. No, I want you to look at yourself, see, for once, how putrid, how ugly . . . '

She felt all that for different reasons, wanted to scream denial at the words, twisted out of his arms and ran for the door, escaping the nearly gentle touch for a brief second. He caught her hair, pulled her back, ignoring the futile scream, and with effortless ease dragged her to the mirror, then with the same ease slammed her head against the glass. Her forehead struck the cold surface with a resounding crack. In the dizziness and pain which followed, she heard the deafening sound of the glass breaking as the mirror shattered in a crunching, groaning impact. Pulled upright, she saw through scarcely focused eyes no image of herself or him, but a web of cracks. Still keeping hold of her with one hand, Charles tore the mirror from the wall and threw it on the floor of the hall. It bounced, the shards of glass split in twinkling, sharp confusion while the oval frame rolled sideways to rest crooked against the wall. Charles pushed Sarah up against the frame of the door, again twisting her face into his.

'Rape, little Fortune? Do you think I wanted only that, something simple, a mere favour? Did want, do want, but only if you were to be another wife, like my own, but not like my own, perfectly pure and good. As I have always wanted, never found.'

He pulled her to the floor, suddenly tender. She, naked; he, fully-clothed and stroking the huge swelling on her forehead, his fingers lingering on the blood oozing from the contusion at her hairline. 'Ah, poor Sarah, sit with me . . .'

Mad, hopelessly mad. In a fog of pain, slumped against the wall, her eyes catching the strewn glass glimmering in the light, she knew he was mad. Hysterical laughter rose in her throat. Madder than his impulses surely, this desire to laugh and stuff her fist in her mouth.

'You know what I did to my wife? No, that's not right, what she did to me, betrayed me, laughed at me. Made me hurt her. I cut her face with my best glass, and then her hands. I didn't mean to cut her hands; hands are blameless, but she tried to cover her face, so I cut them away.'

The voice of him was almost a whine, Sarah's emerged as a rasp.

'Did you kill her?'

'What? No, of course not.' There was a mild, aggrieved surprise at the question. 'I only marked her. To stop her doing that again. I wouldn't ever have killed her; I only punished her. She did the rest.'

'She was your wife. I am no such thing. I owe you nothing.'

'But you are my wife, and you owed me better. You must be punished too, like all the others: you have made men mad.'

He knelt beside her. Then pulled her crouching form away from the door and pushed her to the floor. Sarah cried out briefly as the pieces of glass pierced the skin of her back and shoulders. Impervious, Charles knelt astride, pinning her arms wide for maximum contact with the glass, stopping the mewing sounds of her mouth with his own. Despite the piercing pain, she struggled, feeling the splinters cutting feathery stabs the more she moved, until it was unbearable and the struggles negligible.

'The passion of pain,' murmured Charles, unhurried, unhurt. 'Whenever I punished my wife, I made love to her. But not to you, Porphyria, not to you.'

Her arms had grown numb and she was aware of the floor sticky with blood. When he released his hold, she neither cried nor moved, watched him pick up the largest shard of the old pockmarked glass she had once loved, and draw it down her arm in a thin red trace. Across her belly, scratching rather than cutting, cat tormenting mouse. One long line up her torso, between her breasts, moving to her throat. Then she screamed and screamed, struck back, twisting and turning, feeling the broken glass cracking beneath her. Charles slipped; the triangular shard dug deep into her shoulder with the weight of his hand, and she kicked, struggled, clawed bloody hands into his eyes as he slumped towards her.

If I can push him on to the glass, let him feel this, let him risk his own perfection, stop him being sheltered by my pain, surely it will hurt him through cotton clothes. He will not risk scars ... Charles was grunting with effort, off-balance, nearly falling, holding her wrists to drag them from his face, slowly winning, his expression contorted with fury. One hand was cut from the shard he held. There was a blinding curtain of pain, like glare through a windscreen multiplied by dirt, blood in her eyes and hair running freely from a dozen cuts. She was sinking, drowning in weakness, clawing at him with her back arched away from the vicious glass, losing second by second, warm, slippery, but growing colder and colder. He released one hand; she felt it turning her face to the ground, pressing her cheek towards the splintered glass, playing with her resistance.

I shall die here, she thought. I am going to die. Melodramatic to acknowledge it, unreal to have to imagine at the same time that she who had not wanted to live, did not want to die cut to ribbons without even a blow struck, not even a minor triumph on her own behalf, a death from someone she had never injured, no real ending ... I did not live for this. Her tensed muscles bleeding slower, while the desire to fight suddenly intensified in inverse proportion to the means for trying, a kind of passive indignation mounting slowly.

Then the sudden power of sheer fury, a launching of faded strength as she struck back, kicked, clawed, tried to scream, and felt the impact of his surprise. At the same time, into the midst of them both, there erupted a howling snarling animal, a flurry of red hair, teeth, claws. A mess of three rolling bodies instead of two, and abruptly what had felt like silence was full of sound. The tearing of Charles's cotton sweatshirt, a roar of pain from him, her mouth full of red hair, the dog's and her own, as she rolled away across the glass. Dog was a moving target; Charles could not grasp the writhing shape, but shrieked like a child as he struggled, shifting forward on his knees towards the glass, beating the jaws away with his fist until the teeth took hold for a second time and sank into his wrist. Sarah rolled free, tried to stand, and watched in horror as Charles raised one large hand holding the same shard and chopped repeatedly at the dog's neck. The animal dropped away whimpering, then leapt towards him again, ignoring the glass in the fist, pathetic in wilful ignorance. Sarah could not bear to watch, flung herself at Charles, hanging on to the raised arm with the full force of her weight, knocking him sideways. He slipped, thumped against the wall, twisted out of her grasp and stumbled towards the door, pushing her away in a last violent shove which sent her reeling. She fell and lay still against the supine form of the dog, both of them panting. Below the stairs, she heard a confusion of noise, waited in hope for the sound of the front door slamming, and slid into numbness.

Not my kind of bravery, but I must do as driven by this devil, I who have no trace of violence in me. Through the open door of the flat, from the darkness into the light,

Malcolm saw the glitter of glass, smelt blood, heard Dog howl in pain, before the man in black cannoned through him and down the stairs. Malcolm hesitated for a second, looked forward and back, shouted after the flying figure, and by instinct followed. By the time he reached the front door, he could see the figure beginning to move across the park in a slow trot. In a last practical gesture, Malcolm felt for the keys around his neck, thought fleetingly of the carnage behind him, and ran after the man, better-trained feet tearing at the grass, running as swift as an arrow towards the dark figure which turned and saw him, ran on with lithe speed. Malcolm leapt into the air, caught at the retreating back and crashed the two of them to the ground, rolling in the damp green, with the man's hands beating against his face. One of them was stronger: the blood on the exposed skin was like drying soap, tacky and slimy, difficult to hold or pin to the ground, while the muscles beneath were as hard as steel. In the struggling, panting darkness, Malcolm heard his own voice, furious and low: What have you done, what have you done? Questioning with his own repeated blows which struck that other body into slow submission. He knelt astride, only ceasing his own savage punching long after the end of resistance, aware then of the silence outside their own tortured breathing. In the distance, he heard a police siren, knew it was not for them. Without questioning why, he had realised this to be a private battle, no concern of any other. Sirens were second nature, part of his daily business, they carried his living to his door, but he knew he was beyond their authority, and so was the man who groaned beneath his weight.

In his stirring, and in the sharp movement of the head on the ground, Malcolm dimly recognised his adversary, but before the knowledge of that, was ashamed of his own force, regretted the blows struck beyond those which had been necessary, and in the midst of the dying anger felt guilt and shame. I am no better than any other thug who strikes again and again in mindless fury. Remembered the greater needs inside the building a hundred yards away, still silent, saw there was little he could do with this prisoner bar continue to strike him, stood away, and looked down. Charles turned on his stomach, pulled himself on to his knees, and stood upright slowly himself.

'I know you,' said Malcolm. 'You can wait for your arrest, or leave. I'll find you. I know you.'

The face near his own was smeared and swollen, but even in this transformed state twisted itself into a kind of smile before broken words emerged with breathless deliberation.

'She wouldn't like it, I promise you. Your Porphyria wouldn't like it. Too much to hide . . . ' The voice trailed, but as the figure limped away, Malcolm thought he heard the sound of strange laughter. A childish giggle, sad and gleeful, only ashamed of defeat.

Silence. Moist silence. Spittle running down her chin, and a slow, ponderous drip, drip, drip from the shoulder now leaning against the door. Sarah looked at her feet. Red. Her own blood, Dog's blood, falling to the carpet like a weeping tap. A warm snout pushing against her thigh, urgent whimpering sounds like her own, a tongue making a half-hearted licking against her skin. She put out a sticky hand to the silken head in an automatic stroking, feeling comfort flow into her from the softness of the touch. She moved to stroke the dog's neck, felt the matted fur, sensed the blood, the serious wound. Her mind cleared into urgency: there was someone to rescue, the least she owed, and she tried to stand, like a shameless drunk, looking fixedly at the animal with red streaming down one flank, resisted the temptation to stay still, moving as fast as her limbs would allow.

Skirting the glass clumsily, she stumbled into the bathroom and wrenched two towels from the rail. One she wrapped around herself, dabbed Dog's wound with the other, then tied it round the animal's neck to staunch the flow. Then fell heavily against the door, holding the makeshift collar, waiting for the return of strength.

Into the circle of light, there swam a face of dim familiarity. Who was that? Difficult to tell. The fat man, the thin jogger, some woman's lover. Memory dimmed by blood, but the face was calm and competent, eyes she trusted. 'Please,' she said, 'please ...' The recognition was slow but mutual. There was something in the way she lay curved and naked like a vulnerable foetus which reminded him of another, bolder Sarah Fortune. 'Help us, please ...'

'Shh. Of course I'll help, don't worry ...'

'Is he coming back?'

'Of course not, keep still ...'

'No policemen, please. Don't do that whatever you do, please.'

'Shh,' he said again. 'Anything you say. Doctor though, and a vet ...'

'Yes,' she said wearily. 'Look after that stupid, brave dog.' There was a grim attempt to smile. 'And a vet will do for me too.'

He lifted her into his arms, carried her into the bedroom, noticing the network of cuts, the great gash in the shoulder, the contusion swollen beyond recognition on her forehead. Pain stung her awake as he laid her gently on one side to avoid the fragments of glass which clung to the towelling and the skin. Dear God, how would he explain what had happened, how she and a dog had launched themselves out of a window, some incredible story like that would have to do. The slim body shuddered with relief. 'I'm sorry,' she was muttering. 'Sorry ... Look after the dog. I never meant any of this.' Shaking slightly, a sign of life, even shocked life. Malcolm pulled the duvet round her, then looked at the cut on Dog's neck, a slice to the bone, frighteningly deep, but bleeding less, laid her on her side too, binding the towel tighter. He went to the telephone, listening in the silence to the slight noises of the two wounded. As he dialled, he could hear the muted sounds of Sarah's crying, and even when speaking his appeal for official help, could not resist the single wish, recognised as bizarre as it sprang into his mind through a haze of anxiety, that she would not ask him to leave if ever this was over, not ever, not at all.

CHAPTER THIRTEEN

'Fuck you, Malcolm. Surely you can get her to talk? What kind of bloody lawyer are you? You're a retarded idiot. Born with a brain, can't effing use it. You tell me she's told you she was carved up by Charles Tysall, and his bloody wife's just been washed up with the tide. All this, and then that, currently marked "No Crime", it makes me sick. If she could talk, we'd at least have a bloody angle to weaken him on the death of his wife, but all we've got is a bloody ancient corpse that can't talk, and one healing body who won't talk, won't put on paper what she's said to you. Bloody women. Most of them I know talk all the time. Do something for God's sake. At least get her to promise she'll sign the sheet when she's better.'

A week after the event, Malcolm regretted repeating to Ryan the greater part of what she had told him. She had said as much as she could, and there was more, of a different kind, to come. She had talked when she sat in a hospital bed, receiving a pint of blood through one tube, saline through another, but she had only talked to Malcolm on condition that he repeated to the doctors, who were far from convinced, the story of falling through a window. Now she would not talk anymore, except to him, and would not make any kind of statement identifying her attacker.

In the scepticism born of years of criminal practice, Malcolm could see why. Even five years before, in the days when he had still believed in the ultimate power of law, he would have been the gentle inquisitor, looking for the conviction of an evil man, probing, persuading, warning that truth will out, you may as well comply. In those days he would have said to the reluctant witness, Miss Fortune, you must take an oath and speak, for the sake of catching a breaker of the law who may well hurt another. You must write first, and then speak. Here, take my pen. When Malcolm thought of those he had met in the bowels of the court, refusing to give evidence, until his large and gentle insistence had made them, he blanched. He knew in his heart of hearts that he had persuaded people to believe they would not be hurt in consequence of words said on oath, and that he had never had to see or follow up the beating which would ensue from the friends of the pimp subsequently convicted, or the bruising of the girlfriend of the thief betrayed by her words. This was different, but more or less the same. These days he could see how many were outside the law by sheer influence, could see there were times when it was not worth ruining the life and the trust of one disturbed victim to bring an offender to book. Not even if the offender was Charles Tysall, and not

213

even if other lives hung in the balance. It would make the rickety game of justice one of a life for a life. Especially now.

Malcolm's grasp of the criminal code was so complete he could envisage the trial and all which would follow. Sarah Fortune, pilloried as a greedy whore tormenting a man and suitably punished by falling over a mirror. And, to support the persecution of the witness, no doubt the names and lives of all the lovers, so carefully purloined by the defendant, would be revealed. Malcolm did not know this for sure, but his instincts, and the faithful repetition of Charles's words to Sarah, made him understand the possible extent of his research into her life. Sarah had expected Malcolm to be shocked, but saw no point in hiding anything. He was, after all, both rescuer and criminal lawyer. Malcolm had not been shocked. A life was a life; you did as you could. He did not care what Sarah had done with her body and did not regard it as dishonest. His tolerance was dangerous: a prosecutor was supposed to feel some moral outrage and show at least some sort of belief in his own society's rules, while Malcolm's attitudes, to say nothing of his affections, were going to get him the sack. He had reached that dangerous age when law and punishment mattered less than individuals. In the face of Ryan's fury, he was silent.

'It's all down to you,' Ryan said. 'You and your bloody father, and that woman. And too many secrets. All the secrets you lawyers keep. You aren't normal.'

'Not quite,' Malcolm murmured apologetically. 'And there are other things to consider.'

'Like what?' Ryan shouted. 'Your precious confidentiality

rules, OK? And fuck the rest of us? The fact that you tell me that it would kill your father to step into the witness box and tell on oath what bloody Tysall told him about disfiguring his wife? Or the fact of the reputations of a few other lawyers in the club who've had the privilege with our Sarah? Sorry, guv, your Sarah. What the hell does all of that matter when we've got the chance of nailing a psychopath and a thief?'

'It matters plenty. We're supposed to protect, as well as prosecute, you and I.'

'Leave it out. You might. Protect? At whose expense? Shit. I'm sorry, Mr Cook, I don't get it, and I've had it up to here.' Ryan sketched a line across his own forehead. Malcolm thought of the stitches in Sarah's brow and shuddered slightly, silent against the other's indignation. Ryan tried another tack, the last resort of anger.

'I thought we were friends, Mr Cook, I really did.'

'I'm sorry,' said Malcolm formally.

There was nothing more to say. Ryan left.

Malcolm wished he did not understand it all too well, the anger and the frustration. Wished he had not, unwittingly, confirmed the policeman's view that all lawyers were either charlatans or fools. You're committed to failure, his father had said. Get out of this game, Malcolm; it's bad for the soul. Another hospital bedside, another revealing interview, made brief for Ryan's benefit. And what has your legal game done for you, Father? Sold you a client who has used you as he would a psychoanalyst, abusing you by seeing if he could rely upon you to keep untenable secrets, blackmailing you? Ernest had had the grace to laugh, a short, despairing sound. Well, Son, we who dabble in human lives must take the consequences.

And then there was Sarah, sitting as still as a plant, hiding her wounds in Malcolm's flat, less elegant than her own, more austere, but warm and complete nevertheless. She had not asked to stay, the ambulance had returned her there at his request, and she had not argued, simply demurred. At Malcolm's feet sat Dog, recovering from a fretwork of stitches, stable by his side, although in the time of Sarah's constant presence, the loyalties had become divided. Not divided as such, said Sarah, simply multiplied. After all, she saved me; she can't be stand-offish now, although she should bite me if she had any sense, since I got her those stitches. But for all the ease, Sarah was watchful like a cat, residing in the home of another because of a need, a weakness in herself she resented all the time. He wished she would simply accept the need, possibly with the same calmness with which she had accepted the serious injury, the permanently scarred forehead, still clear headed, obstinate to the end.

'Why won't you talk to the police?' he had asked, to establish an answer he knew full well after her clear account to him of the evening of her attack and all the two years which had preceded it.

'Because it would do more harm than good in the long run. And because I know the limitations of evidence. I don't object to the ruining of my unimportant reputation, or falling from respectability, but I won't risk the same for anyone else. I might not be an innocent, but the lovers were, in their own way. So is your father. Charles Tysall knows very well

I wouldn't risk exposing them. I don't believe anything as clumsy as the due process of law could catch him anyway.'

He accepted that as he accepted all she had done with her life in the meantime between that single encounter of two years before which had been etched on his mind ever since. It no longer occurred to him to judge, condemn, or even wonder whether a thing was illegal or immoral: he could only see whether it was well-intended, harmful or not, quite different distinctions. Malcolm believed in nothing, but he knew that he loved her. He knew and wanted the heart of what he loved. Whatever had been done with the body did not matter. Pasts did not matter, only futures. There would be a long wait, but he had time. It crossed his mind what they would do for money once he had survived his forthcoming interview with the Chief Crown Prosecutor, to explain his harbouring of a refugee, as well as explaining his own refusal to contribute to the evidence, but that too was irrelevant.

Charles Tysall had sat for many hours in a dim interview room with a faceless Superintendent, a note-taking Sergeant, and his own, newly recruited solicitor, a man with a face like a weasel. Horses for courses: one solicitor to whom one confesses; another, eminently corruptible, in whose presence one says nothing of any importance at all. Whilst voluble Ryan had acquainted the interrogators with the reasons for the bandages on the hands of the suspect, the marks to his face and the slight stiffness to the walk, it was not their mandate to question him on the basis of hearsay evidence, or any evidence at all of events so recent. They had been removed from

217

the confines of Norfolk to ask their suspect about older history than that. There was a sharp demarcation zone in their inquiries: what the man had done in London was London's concern, while the discoveries of Norfolk, confirmed by a Knightsbridge dentist, were theirs. As a concession to other inquiries, Ryan was allowed as inside observer, and as the greatest concession of all, Superintendent Bailey was allowed to ask some of the questions.

'When did you last see your wife, Mr Tysall?'

'Two and a half years ago. We quarrelled, and she left me. She had had an accident.'

'What kind of accident?'

'Domestic.'

'I see. Were you involved in that accident?'

'My client does not have to answer that question,' interrupted the weasel.

'The choice is his,' said Bailey, well used to the interference of legal representatives, while the Norfolk officers shuffled with indignation. In their own county, lawyers were more co-operative. 'I'll ask again. Were you involved, sir?' It was an automatic reflex to call Charles sir. In Norfolk, anyone not actually on a charge was not called otherwise. They were not fools, but they were invariably courteous. Charles was immobile, urbane and alert. Wearing that look the Superintendent recognised, and which told him a man would tell him nothing.

'If you don't mind, I shall take my solicitor's advice and not answer that question. Except to say I was aware of her accident, and how much it distressed her, as did our relationship, which was not happy. She sought treatment for her injuries;

no doubt you will find evidence of that, but she made no complaint. It was not a criminal matter. Then she left. She told me she was going back to America. From whence she came. I did not pursue her.'

'What about money? What was she going to do about that? I presume she was financially dependent on you?'

'You presume correctly. Who knows what she planned?' He spread his hands, still expressive, even in bandages. 'If she had wanted money she would have asked, but she had the deeds of our house in Norfolk, in her name, a valuable property. I regarded that as her settlement.'

'Minor, for a man of your means.'

'Surely. But had she asked more, I would have complied.'

No you would not, Bailey had concluded, you would have fought tooth and nail to deny her a penny, because she had abandoned you. But he allowed the polite flow to continue.

'In any event, she had credit cards. I closed and paid off the accounts six months after she left.'

'And you made no effort to find her?'

'No. I find it preferable to sustain defection in silence, Superintendent. What would I have achieved by looking?'

'Peace of mind, perhaps?'

'My mind was not troubled. Besides, it is constantly engaged. I am a very busy man.'

No trace of her in the man's flat ('Will you look at this place, look at all this stuff? He must be loaded . . .'), scene of crime specialists beginning their task in hope, ending in frustration. Not an inch of carpet older than a year, nothing more than sanitised cleanliness everywhere, some long, dark

219

hairs beneath the bed, that was all. Charles's address book and all his confidential correspondence locked in a safe in the weasel's office. The letter from his dead wife, informing him of her intentions and announcing the incriminating letters she would leave on her person explaining quite clearly the reasons for a self-inflicted death, had long since perished on a Norfolk bonfire.

There was nothing then, apart from a drowned body discovered in a sand-bank. And a placid man, with an alibi for all possible days eighteen months before, when he could show he had not left London for a single day, who knew he would not be charged with murder or anything like.

Disposal by hired help, the interrogator thought. Contracted death, hopeless, but not as cruel as the total absence of grief which stung the questioner most.

'Did you love your wife, Mr Tysall?' An announcement of a question, designed to shock, if only a little.

'What do you mean?'

'What I said. Love her, the way normal human beings do. Did you?' The colour drained from a pale face, leaving the bruises livid. There was a twitching of the limbs, a brief contortion of the features into a peculiar mask of anger and grief. The weasel stirred to restrain his client.

'Love her?' said the face loudly. 'Love her? Of course I loved her. Better than anything else in the world.'

Silence had fallen. Only the slight scratch of the pen on lined paper as the note-taker, unperturbed, wrote, 'better than anything in the world', finished with a slight flourish before the pen dropped.

'I think,' said the weasel, 'my client has had enough for now. Anything else I regard as oppressive.'

'Oppressive?' said Sarah, 'Is that what Superintendent Bailey told you?'

'Yes,' said Malcolm. 'He's the only one left who'll speak to me.'

'Oh, Malcolm.' She pulled Dog towards her in a gesture of affectionate despair. It's me who's oppressive. I seem to have isolated you. Nothing good has come to you ever since we met. Your job is at risk. You don't see friends. I've been a sort of curse on your life.'

Over the weeks, their conversation had assumed an easy, joking banter, hiding nothing.

'What do you mean, no good has come from you? Look at my slender figure.' He pirouetted in the room, grinning, a touch of the old Malcolm, ready to joke as a more dignified buffoon. 'That was you, though you may not know it. Then there's Dog, an indirect credit to you. What more could man owe woman? Friends I don't miss, except for the few I hope either to acquire or keep: Bailey, Helen West. And you.'

'Friends? Friends have to be equal, and whatever you say the balance between us is all in your favour. I owe you everything, including wanting to stay alive. And I'm hardly suitable material for a friend. Not even an acquaintance or relative to give me ballast. And, as an extra credential, two years behind the mask of respectable prostitution.'

'Do you regret that?'

She hesitated. 'No. I was always on the outside; being what

I was didn't seem different. I would only regret if I had hurt anyone, so no, I don't regret it.'

'Good, I should respect you less if you did. Is there anything you do regret?'

'Of course. Like not having the comfort of moral beliefs. Making such an obsession of love, and such a cynical matter of its absence. Not knowing you a long time ago. Not having a baby. Or a dog.'

He was standing by the window watching the park settling for the evening. Dying sunlight played on his features, turning the thick hair blue-black, making his eyes deeper set and his profile sharper. Malcolm was long and lean, strangely authoritative and utterly relaxed in his own home with this company. Sarah regarded him with covert affection and respect, tinged with a vague longing she was frightened to show. The man deserved far better than this.

'It's time I left you in peace, Malcolm. Summer's turned autumn. I've been here six weeks. Too long.'

He continued to look into the park, examined the view, shrugged his shoulders.

'You must do exactly as you wish. Leave me in peace? If you must. But if you leave, I should not be in peace.'

'No,' she said softly. 'Nor would I.'

He spoke as much to himself as to her. 'Outsiders, both of us. We arrived at the outside by different routes, as unlikely a pair of lawyers as you could hope to find. Quite indifferent to the status quo we are paid to preserve. We may as well be on a different planet from the rest.'

'We are.'

'Well,' he said diffidently, 'it might not be a bad idea to circulate earth in company. I've always wanted a garden.'

'And I the dog.'

'Ah, if you had had either dog or child, you might not have had the lovers.' He was laughing now, and he turned back towards her, squatted by her chair and took her hand. 'So you may stay a little longer?'

'Please. Although I don't see why you ask.'

'Let's see how we go.'

She stroked the blue-black hair, feeling strength, new blood in her veins after a ritual bloodletting, she thought. A strange sensation after three years of caring for nothing, like the bends in the blood of a diver coming up from the very deep in search of air.

He sat beside her and kissed her lightly, a first time kiss.

'What shall we do?' she asked, smiling.

'Well, by degrees, we could shorten the distance between your room and mine. After that, travel hopefully. Far better than arriving.'

She leant into him, conscious of the warmth of him, the care he took with her, wondering why he should, but grateful.

'And if Tysall should come back, not here but elsewhere? Charles is on my conscience. Not him, but the harm he can do and I have not prevented.'

'We shall have to see,' said Malcolm. 'He may be beyond the law, but not beyond his own demons. He may destroy himself.'

'In rage, do you think?'

'Oh no. In cold blood or arrogance. What he may do cannot be helped. We have to fight our own battles.'

'Is that what outsiders do?'

'It is.'

'I do not want him to suffer. I don't want anyone to suffer, I want to believe people can change the course of their lives.'

'We shall prove that they can.'

Silence fell. Dog moved, and slept again.

'Malcolm, I have never trusted anyone before. Or not for so long that I can't remember what it is like.'

'Nor I. But we shall learn, you and I.'

'Shall we? Am I, at least, not beyond hope?'

'I don't know. I don't believe, now, that anyone is.' He smiled suddenly. 'But we have to try. We have our responsibilities, you know. There's a dog to bring up . . .'

She looked back at him, echoing the old mischief.

'Oh yes, of course. I forgot. That settles it then.'

Never trust a lawyer, or a copper, and trust the court least of all. Ryan was pushing his maverick trail out for battle rather than solutions, back on the course of unfinished business. Dead Mrs Tysall and the vision of Annie freshened by his own impotence and a fair degree of new guilt. I hate you, you bastard. If I do not have you, I do not sleep and cannot get on with my life. And I am angry in my bones for turning away, when I, more than anyone, should have kept on watching.

'It's Mr Tysall, isn't it?'

Charles looked up. The bruises had disappeared, the face was cold and distant, and although the level of sublime self-assurance was less, the responses were as controlled as they had always been.

224

'You don't need to ask, Mr Ryan. You know perfectly well.'

'May I sit down for a minute?'

'I'd rather you didn't, but I can't stop you.'

Ryan sat, pretending a nonchalance he did not feel in this airy coffee shop where he had followed Charles and watched him eat a frugal breakfast. One small croissant, three dark coffees.

'I was looking for Ted Plumb, Mr Tysall.'

'I don't believe you, but you look in vain. Mr Plumb has disappeared.'

'People connected with you have that habit, sir, don't they?' Ryan remarked conversationally.

'Yes. I have to concede that. Especially wives. But Edward's disappearance is not of that kind. He will reappear, like the proverbial bad penny.'

'I see. Not like the wife, then.'

'As I said. But she reappeared too.'

Ryan sipped the coffee he had brought from his own table. In the weeks intervening since the discovery of Elisabeth Tysall, his anger had faded into a dull curiosity, blunted by a sense of futility. He required some kind of reaction from this calm face more than he needed explanations. Ryan was learning that there need not be any explanations, but it irked him, the powerful frustration flowing from a man who was beyond hurting, whose physical wounds healed with the same even speed as the rest, and he wanted above all to needle a response. He wanted to prickle and hurt like those little pieces of glass he had seen in Sarah Fortune's flat before the doors were closed against him. Not your case, DS Ryan,

225

not anyone's case, thank you. Oh, Mr Tysall, you are beyond the law, but not beyond suffering, surely, nor quite outside all those little devils which trouble me. Besides, I'm curious. I saw you react, just the once, when you announced you had loved your wife. Perhaps you did, like I love mine. Like I loved Annie. You were hurting then; I want to see it again, you bastard. Then I shan't feel so useless. I hate you, Charles Tysall, you stinking mixed-up coward. Hate you for failing to understand you at all, and because you didn't even have the guts to kill anyone. You just made them want to do it themselves and sent me on a goosechase. You've made a monkey of me, Charles old boy, so I shall try to needle you with the unanswered question you do not seem to have considered.

'Do you have to sit here, Mr Ryan? Surely you have other duties? I don't have to speak to you.'

'Shan't keep you, sir. You don't have to answer, but I hoped you might, and if you do, it isn't for the record . . . One question in my head, the rest I can live with . . . I have to, don't I?' Charles nodded grimly. ' . . . But your wife, Mr Tysall sir, Elisabeth. One thing defeats me. It seems she may have killed herself, but who,' here he paused for effect, 'buried her? Dug her in, I mean,' he added to emphasise the point.

Charles stirred and clasped long fingers together, faced luminous eyes on the broad features next to his, then turned his attention to the half-finished cup of coffee, the hand holding it trembling slightly, Ryan noticed with satisfaction.

'Buried, Mr Ryan? The sand buried her, or so I understand. A natural process: the force of water moving sand to cover an intrusion. Maybe she died in a natural hollow and was covered. No one mentioned burial, not in the terms I understand.'

'No?' said Ryan. 'Fancy that. But then you were being questioned about her disappearance, not her burial. I promise you she was buried, sir, in a bank which split open later. Buried deep, sir, or there would have been nothing left to see. There was nothing natural about the burial, sir, human hand, not nature's. You could always go and look, sir, ask the locals if you don't believe me. Someone definitely dug a hole and put her in it . . .'

'No,' said Charles, cup crashing against saucer, his voice unnaturally loud.

'Yes, they did,' said Ryan, grinning his wolfish grin, teeth on the jugular, pleased to have found the weak spot with his usually faulty instinct. 'Yes they bloody did. Sir.'

Charles's right hand clenched the edge of the table, a white scar on his dark skin glowing against the wood.

'So,' Ryan went on relentlessly, pursuing his advantage, 'she didn't just fade away, did she? Someone had their hands all over that lily-white body right at the end, and not yours either, I suppose. Poor Elisabeth, always partial to a bit of the other, wasn't she? I hope he was a good strong man, well-endowed, if you see what I mean. Gentle, passionate and sensitive with it; you know, all the things a woman could ever have wanted . . . Hope he made her scream before he buried her . . . I can see it all, one last night together on the sands: Elisabeth darling, I'll show you what a man can do . . .'

Charles choked, the pale skin blotched. He pushed at the table and half ran for the door. A waiter stepped into his path and stepped aside, seeing the rapt expression of a man on the verge of nausea. Ryan turned to watch the departure, then resumed his cold coffee, suddenly unperturbed. He sat back, smiling. All right then, no answers at all, but at least he'd kicked where it hurt, clever enough to have found the spot. More than one way to skin a cat. The bastard. He signalled the waiter.

'More coffee please. And don't worry,' he jerked his head in the direction of the door, 'I'll pay for his breakfast.' Then I'll go home and sort out the wife, he added to himself, catching his healthy reflection in a mirror on the wall.

Who had buried Porphyria, stoked her into the mud in her final, obscene abandonment? Charles arrived at the quayside during the Saturday business of mid-afternoon. The sense of holiday was gone, winter in the air, stragglers peering at boats, leaning over the sea-wall to feed the birds in the channels; then disappearing into the warmth of the cafés and amusement arcades. Fish and chip front down to the east end of the harbour reserved for fishermen, where the wind blew colder and the water was relatively empty, the tide low, leaving acres of mud and sand exposed between the swift channels of water running in between the banks. He had witnessed this scene before, never with the same fascination. Elisabeth it was who loved the sea, the peculiar mystery of this double-edged landscape, at once a bleak view of colourful earth and muddy rivulets, filling with tide, until it seemed as if the ocean had come to land leaving only the slightest trace of tufty ground. The surfaces above the channels were covered with sea-lavender, a faded but vivid carpet as far as his eye could see. Cardinal's purple, Charles thought, a pall for a coffin, but I never saw her buried.

He began to walk down the old stone steps of the quay wall and across the mud where boats lay like beached whales waiting for water. Absently, he removed his shoes before wading across the nearest channel to the opposite bank, surprised at the coldness of the water and the strength of the current pulling around his calves, flowing inland. It was all innocuous, peaceful and calm in the stiff breeze. He walked on, skirting the glittering water, feeling sand beneath his feet.

'Mister!'

There was a small boy crossing his path, walking back purposefully towards the quay, stopping Charles's progress towards the skyline of the distance.

'Mister, don't go far up the creeks, Mister. The tide's turned, see?'

He looked at the child with the contempt he had always reserved for children, angry to be disturbed by a human voice.

'What do you mean, boy? Get out of my way. There's other people further out.'

'Coming back, though, not going out. They're coming back in, don't you see?'

Charles did not understand. Nor did he wish to know the child's nonsense, but the boy stood firm, ready to elaborate his explanation. Irritably, he pushed the slight figure out of his path and walked on.

He had in his mind the picture they had shown him of where she had been found. It was imperative to discover

229

the place now, not later or another day but now. In the slow churning thoughts which had governed his actions since the morning, there had been one burning question demanding immediate answer. Who had buried her, intervened like a lover in that last chapter of her life. He needed to discover the place. To ensure Ryan was wrong. Once he had seen the place he would surely find what he needed to know. That there had been no lecherous undertaker willed to Elisabeth's side in final infidelity or in death. There would be no peace, no sleep until he discovered that patch of sandy earth, and found it innocent. The wind was growing colder. He moved quickly.

The boy was faster, ran after him, caught up, pulled his arm.

'Don't go, Mister,' he was shouting. 'Tide'll be high today. Too much east wind. And there's nothing to see.'

Charles looked down at the anxious face, seeing nothing but obstruction, interference and sheer insolence. He raised his arm and struck the child a casual blow to the head as he would have thrashed at a branch obstructing his path. Unprepared, the boy sprawled sideways into the sand with a grunt of surprise, scrambling up within seconds, ready to fight back. But he saw that the man had moved on without a backward glance, and his own eyes narrowed as he rubbed his jaw, felt the beginnings of a dull pain and involuntary tears in his eyes. By his side, slow to protect, a small dog barked anxiously and licked his hand.

Pain turned to anger. The small guardian of the creeks saw the long figure striding into the distance, walking along the banks, following the path where he himself would have taken the boat, disappearing from view as the very last of the walkers returned back to the harbour-wall. The sky was turning ugly grey in the last of the daylight. Let him, then. Don't interfere or tell him his business.

Don't tell anyone else either.

'Come on, boy,' he said. 'Time to go home.'

'Where would we go,' said Sarah to Malcolm, 'if we did not have to live here?'

'To the sea I think. I find it soothing.'

'And dangerous.'

He put his arm round her with the familiarity of a brother. 'We can and we will change our lives. The privilege of being human. Nothing is safe, but nothing is hopeless either. Look in the mirror.' He hugged, less brotherly, turned her to face the new mirror on the wall. 'What do you see?'

'You and I against the world?'

'Yes.'

'We can do anything then,' said Sarah.

Have you read them all?
Entire backlist now in ebook

Have you read them all?
Entire backlist now in ebook

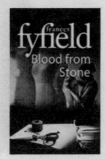